# The Senator's Mistress

## THE WOMAN WHO KNEW TOO MUCH

ANNA RAINS

Copyright © 2025 by Anna Rains

Paperback: 978-1-967820-09-2
eBook: 978-1-967820-10-8
Library of Congress Control Number: 2025908234

All rights reserved. No part of this publication may be reproduced, distributed, or transmitted in any form or by any electronic or mechanical means, without the prior written permission of the publisher, except in the case of brief quotations embodied in critical reviews and certain other noncommercial uses permitted by copyright law.

This is a work of nonfiction.

Ordering Information:

Prime Seven Media
518 Landmann St.
Tomah City, WI 54660

Printed in the United States of America

# Acknowledgement

I would like to thank Amber Stone of Prime Seven Media, my publishers, who has been there for me, encouraged and come up with ideas for titles and front covers. Her belief in my work has inspired me to concentrate on getting my books completed.

Also, must thank two friends, both Anne's, who have read through my work and helped with the editing for which I am very grateful.

# Chapter 1

The safe deposit box crashed to the ground, spilling its contents across the floor. Carrie looked up and stared into the eyes of the man who had opened the box. The jewellery scattered everywhere. One piece was a beautiful gold and ruby bracelet. Carrie recognised it instantly.

"Where did you get that?" she almost whispered.

Without saying a word, the man grasped her arm, twisting it viciously. Carrie whimpered in fear as his dark and angry eyes swept over her. The man let go of Carrie's wrist and knocked her violently to the ground.

"You open your mouth and you're dead too!"

He left quickly, leaving Carrie terrified and bruised, so frightened she rolled herself into a tight ball, unable to call out for help. One glance at the bracelet and she'd known he must have been involved in the brutal killing of the old lady she had befriended. It was of such an unusual design there was no mistaking it. The old lady had called it 'Dragon's Breath'.

Over the past two years, this same old lady had rambled on about her life – revealing secrets of other deaths and scandals and hints of dirty dealing of past Presidents and governments. Initially, Carrie took some of her stories with a pinch of salt, but as she became closer to her, she was convinced that the old lady had known much more than she should have done. Some of these secrets were written down in journals and papers currently hidden away in a safe deposit box belonging to Carrie, only a few feet away – including facts about the inexplicable death of one of the former world's leading actresses, Maizie Fraser, some forty years earlier. It had been reported that this Hollywood movie star had committed suicide, but Carrie's old lady had more than hinted she'd been murdered to shut her up.

Two deaths were probably already connected, and she was terrified she might be the next victim.

# Chapter 2

Three years before Carrie's terrifying meeting with the man in the safe deposit box department, Carrie Swallow looked up from the computer on the counter of the Savings and Loan where she worked in Southern California. At this point, she hadn't the slightest idea that the future friendship with the old lady, who was standing on the other side of her desk, would end with one of them being violently murdered and the other fleeing for her life.

Carrie smiled as she reached out for the passbook being offered to her. "Hi, how can I help you?" she asked courteously, while smiling to herself at the sight of this astonishing woman.

The elderly lady in front of her was strung with quantities of jewellery. She had at least eight rings on her fingers, and when she handed over her passbook, bracelets on both wrists jangled together. Several chains, necklaces, and some long dangly earrings completed her ensemble.

"Hi Carrie," she answered, peering at the name badge on Carrie's smart navy business suit. Offering the young woman a very thick envelope, she said, "I'd like to deposit this money in my account."

"Thanks, Ms Bushnell," replied Carrie as she opened the book and read the name inside. "How much is it you want to deposit?"

"I don't know, Honey. I haven't counted it. I just collected it up from round my apartment and thought I'd better bring it down."

Carrie was surprised, but the bank was located near a large retirement community where many elderly, and some extremely eccentric, people lived.

"Right, Ms Bushnell, we'd better count it then."

Ms Bushnell smiled again, and Carrie instinctively responded to the old lady with bright blue eyes, pure white hair, and dressed in clothes far more suited to a much younger woman. On this occasion, she was wearing a 'tank top', pink jeans, and trainers that many a teenager would have envied. Round her waist was a belt covered in diamante and sequins. These, along with the jewellery, presented a very odd picture.

As if reading her mind, the old lady smiled, her eyes twinkling and said, "Oh I know, Honey, my clothes are not at all what most women of my age wear, but I don't care what anyone thinks – I feel really comfortable dressed this way."

"I think you look fantastic! It's great to meet someone like you," responded the younger woman as she sorted out the dollar notes into respective values.

"Well, Carrie, I was never pretty like you, and so, in order to get myself noticed, I've always dressed oddly," she said as she looked at the tall attractive young woman busy counting her money.

Late-twenties, Ms Bushnell guessed as she watched Carrie. Must have been an attractive youngster. She was right. Carrie, as a child, had been all brown skinny arms and legs, with an engaging open face sprinkled with freckles. Clear grey eyes had gazed at the world with extreme curiosity. She had been one of those children who could not be happy with the sort of half answers some adults were inclined to give. She would go on asking questions until she got a satisfactory reply. Her mind hadn't changed, but the scrawny kid had grown up into a tall, beautiful woman with long, shapely legs and a body that could well have graced the cat walks of Paris or New York. It was only later that Ms Bushnell learnt about Carrie's disastrous marriage at the age of nineteen.

"One hundred and twenty-two thousand, one hundred and fifty-six dollars, Ms Bushnell," Carrie said, interrupting the old lady's thoughts. "Do you want it all in this account, or would you like to open a longer-term, higher interest rate account for some of it?"

"No, just put it all in there for today. Perhaps next time I'm in, I'll think about changing it over."

Carrie was curious about why she should have so much loose money in her home, but was too polite to ask. It was only later when she began to learn more about this astonishing woman that she realised this was perhaps one of the *least* surprising things about her.

Carrie completed the transaction and returned the passbook. As she said goodbye, she thought – What a pity my father died last year, he would really have loved to meet her!

A great sadness swept over her as she thought about her father. She and her father had been very close after her mother, a former Australian, had run off with her best friend's husband and moved out of State when Carrie was fifteen and a half. Carrie and her English father, who had brought the family from England when Carrie was only four, had lived together until she married just before her twentieth birthday. He'd done his best to dissuade her from throwing herself away on Bill Swallow – 'a waster if ever I saw one' was his comment, but she was adamant she knew what she was doing. It was only after the inevitable divorce that Carrie agreed her dad had been right all along – and she moved back in with him. A terrible crash had taken away the life of her wonderful father, leaving her feeling very alone. It had happened on the very winding road leading up to Big Bear and Lake Arrowhead and had been caused by a maniac driving too fast.

She remembered her father telling her as she grew up to, "Keep your British accent" because Americans love to hear it. "It'll help you in business as you get older", he added.

Ah well, thought Carrie briefly, as she dragged her mind back to Ms Bushnell, at least I will make Olivia laugh when we meet up on my way home this evening for a cocktail. After that, on the weekend just before the long Labour Day weekend, she was far too busy to think any more about her father or the unusual old lady.

# Chapter 3

Carrie and her friend Olivia Richards met at the Tortilla Ranch restaurant. Both loved meeting at this particular place with its large fans slowly moving air around their heads. Big exotic plants gently swayed with the soft breeze and made the whole room feel like a tropical forest.

"Hi Olivia," called out Carrie, when she arrived a little after her friend.

"Hi Carrie, it's great to see you. I've only just got here."

They sat down at a small cocktail table in the cool, low-lit bar area. Neither of them wanted a meal, but the margaritas served with homemade tortilla chips covered in thick melted cheese to nibble at were worth coming for.

The two had met in grade school and had been friends ever since. Olivia, shorter and blond, had always envied her friend's height and beautiful, long, dark hair, but had never let it stop her from becoming best buddies. She had been one of Carrie's bridesmaids at the ill-fated wedding and had gone through the highs and lows when Carrie decided to divorce her rotten husband.

The two women ordered a large margarita each and a plateful of tortillas to share. The drinks arrived in what Olivia said looked like 'bird baths'. As Carrie licked away some of the salt round the rim, Olivia raised her glass and wished her 'a great weekend'.

"Umm. Wow – that tastes great! There's nothing like a cold margarita after a busy day at work, is there?"

"I agree!" responded Olivia. "Fantastic."

They sat back in their comfortable chairs while they talked about their respective jobs. Carrie told Olivia about her meeting with the old lady, at which Olivia laughed as Carrie knew she would. Then Olivia told Carrie about the people she had moved into a new home that day.

"You know, when the husband said he must have a triple garage and he didn't care what the house looked like, I thought it was because he was really into cars – but no – when I turned up with my housewarming gift, I found him pushing a half-built airplane into one side of the garage, in place of any of his vehicles!"

"Into home-built airplanes, is he?" asked Carrie knowledgeably.

"Yeh – that's right. His long-suffering wife said the airplane took priority!"

The two girls chatted on for about an hour and a half before going their separate ways – although they were meeting up the next morning for a day on the beach followed by a barbecue at the home of some mutual married friends. They called out goodnight, and Carrie drove off in her red Mustang heading home.

Wow, the freeway is really busy tonight, she thought as she hit the on ramp. Everybody will be heading to the beach cities for the September Labour Day weekend. One last weekend away before getting down to work again, and the kids return to school after the long summer vacation.

She drove carefully, conscious that she and Olivia had each had two large margaritas. She couldn't go fast anyway, as she headed south for a few miles between Laguna Hills and Crown Valley Parkway. Crown Valley eventually came out on the Coast Highway, where Carrie turned north towards the home she owned in South Laguna. She had been lucky to find the delightful two-bedroomed house. An old school friend had mentioned selling it because she was moving 'back east,' and Carrie had snapped it up.

Carrie had been at a low point when it became available several months after her father's death. She'd remained for a while in the large four-bedroomed home they'd shared in Monarch Bay, between South Laguna and Dana Point, but after his death, she hated the big modern house overlooking the Pacific Ocean. It was filled with so many memories of her life with her father. Fortunately, the buyers had moved into Orange County from New England and were happy to purchase most of the furniture, which was ideally suited to Southern California.

Carrie happily moved into her new home, which had actually been built about sixty years before – old by Californian standards. Her friends called it 'funky'. It certainly had loads of character – and the price reflected that! She'd only been able to afford it after she'd sold her father's home.

Now, with a feeling of pleasure, she parked her car on the driveway in front of her home, checked her mailbox for any mail, smiling as she took out a letter from her godmother in England, and let herself into her cool, dimly lit home.

# Chapter 4

After the initial meeting across the counter of the Savings and Loan, Carrie and Ms Bushnell gradually got to know each other very well.

It was about six months from the time they first met that Carrie became concerned when she realised, she hadn't seen the old lady for two or three weeks. Ms Bushnell always came in on a Friday afternoon to deposit or withdraw money. At first, Carrie thought she must have missed her because she had been moved from her position as teller and was now working in the Safe Deposit department. The department was always busy with over ten thousand boxes, and sometimes the five girls working in that area of the bank hardly had time to go on a coffee break. However, upon enquiry, she discovered that nobody had seen her for a while and as Carrie laughingly said, "You couldn't miss Ms Bushnell – she's definitely one of the world's most colourful characters!"

When the following Friday came and went, and still no sign of the old lady, Carrie looked up her telephone number and called her. Ms Bushnell admitted she hadn't been well, and so Carrie offered to help with shopping or whatever else she needed doing. That afternoon, after work, Carrie visited the supermarket armed with a long list of groceries and necessities for the old lady and took them to her apartment.

Upon arrival, she was invited to 'come on in'. An opened bottle of wine and a couple of glasses were ready on a low table in the sitting room.

"Help yourself while I put these things away," Ms Bushnell called as she waved her hand towards the bottle.

Carrie did as she suggested and poured out a glass of Californian Zinfandel for each of them. While she waited for the Ms Bushnell to finish what she was doing, Carrie looked at her surroundings with amused appreciation. The apartment reflected the old lady's approach to her clothing – *over the top!*

First there were books everywhere – much to Carrie's surprise, she hadn't envisioned this unusual woman as a great reader. It wasn't just fiction either, there were books on travel, autobiographies, political works and a number of biographies devoted to Maizie Fraser, the former well known Hollywood actress.

Lamps with Tiffany glass shades, several chess sets of various designs, made from ivory, carved wood and different colours of jade; overstuffed chairs, piles of cushions and vases filled with real and artificial flowers crowded the surfaces of everything. No wonder she found so much money hidden here amongst her things, thought Carrie, reminiscing back to their first meeting at the bank. She was still enjoying looking round this extraordinary room when Ms Bushnell came to join her.

Over their first glass of wine the old lady asked Carrie to call her RT. She explained that RT stood for Rose Tranton, her Christian names. Rose for her mother and Tranton was an old family name of her father's.

"Rose Bushnell," she said disgustedly, "fancy calling me Rose, with the surname Bushnell! Of course, at school, I was known as rose bush! That's why I changed it to RT. I never married and so I'm still Rose Bush."

Carrie laughed at the expression on her face but agreed that although Rose was a very pretty name, she could understand why the other girls at school had teased her.

They chatted on for about an hour before Carrie said she had to leave.

"A hot date?" enquired RT.

"A date, yes, but I don't know how hot. I think he is keen enough but I'm not ready to get hitched up again yet. His name is Daniel Bentley, though he's usually called Dan and he's an airline pilot who lives in Vancouver, so I only see him when he's on an overnight down here."

"Well Honey, have a good evening anyway."

The two ladies agreed to meet one evening during the following week for an early meal and Carrie departed.

After this initial meeting the two women met regularly, either at one of their homes, or at one of the prolific restaurants in the area. Sometimes venturing as far south as Dana Point or San Clemente, or north to Corona del Mar and Newport Beach. One of their favourite fish restaurants overlooked the harbour of Newport Beach. They loved going early to get a table right at the front, where they would watch the sun go down, dropping so fast over the horizon you could almost feel as if it was being pulled into the ocean by a piece of string. As the last remnants of the sun disappeared, so the lights all around the harbour came on. They watched boats leisurely making their way back to their moorings with their sails dropping as the skippers turned on the engines to motor the last half a mile or so.

Both agreed they were an odd couple. RT could easily have been Carrie's grandmother. As the months went by, they got to know a great deal about each other. On one of the earliest evenings, they went out for dinner, RT began to tell Carrie about her extraordinary life.

"My father was a descendant of the Pilgrim Fathers and very proud of it of course. I was born in the small town of Albany in New York State where my father was local mayor, but I spent a lot of time with my grandmother in Rhode Island. He'd won the office on the 'Mayflower ticket' and went on to greater things as the years went by."

RT paused while the waiter took their orders before continuing. "I was the middle one of three sisters and was a tomboy from day one. They were both much prettier than me."

Carrie protested but RT interrupted, "No, I really was unattractive as a child – plump, spotty and sulky. It's no wonder my sisters got all the attention. They would be wheeled out to sing and play the piano while I was stuck with an extremely strict English nanny." She laughed as she added quickly, "Sorry Carrie, I hadn't forgotten you are English. I think Nanny Goodman must have grown up in a school out of a Dicken's book. She was very evil and often locked me in my room for hours without food or anything to drink when she thought I had misbehaved. She didn't like it when I made fun of her name and called her Nanny Badwoman!"

Carrie laughed with her but inside she felt very sad. "What about your parents? Didn't they intervene?"

"No. They wanted us to grow up to become debutantes and marry well and be people they could be proud of. I didn't fit my mother's ideas of 'cute kid'."

Carrie topped up both their glasses and signalled the waiter to bring another bottle. RT would drink most of it as she had a very strong head and besides Carrie was driving.

"When I was at kindergarten my teachers were always complaining that I preferred larking around with the boys. I loved climbing trees and was always tearing my clothes instead of playing with dolls like the other girls. My mom gave up in despair and stopped buying me girlish things. She concentrated on bringing up my sisters. I called her *mom* to annoy her. She really hated it and told me so many times to refer to her as Mother!" RT said with a cynical tone in her voice.

Carrie sat quietly hoping to encourage the old lady to open up further.

"When I was six my father became an assistant to the State Senator for Pennsylvania, and we moved to Washington D.C. It was then my ambitious father began to dream about even higher office – even running for the Presidency one day. You know, he never forgave me for my future behaviour. He reckoned that I cost him the chance. The things I did later in life were widely written about in everything from the National Enquirer to Time Magazine. He hated me for the scandals I caused."

"What happened after you moved to Washington D.C.?" enquired Carrie.

"Well, I was torn away from my friends in Albany and behaved even worse. In desperation, my parents decided to pack me off for a long visit to my grandparents' house in Rhode Island. Actually, that was the happiest time in my childhood. I adored my grandmother. I think I took after her because she'd been very wild as a young woman. My great grandfather tried to marry her off to an American aristocratic prat. She was a considerable heiress in her own right and spoiled all his plans by running off with the handsome son of the local doctor."

Carrie laughed and remarked that the American New England descendants of the Mayflower were probably even more snobbish than the English Aristocracy.

"It was a very happy marriage, he was the doctor's son, and although my grandfather was wonderful in his own way, he was considered totally beneath 'Miss Trenton, a descendant of Salem, Massachusetts'."

Carrie interrupted, "I'm sure the English royals have turned up their noses at some of the newcomers who have married into the family over the years, starting with Princess Margaret and Anthony Armstrong Jones."

"At least in England they give them titles to cover up their humbler backgrounds," retorted RT. "I wish I'd been allowed to stay with my grandparents. I remember riding in the back of my grandmother's automobile behind her stately chauffeur. We would go down to the waterfront to watch the fishing boats come in and then take tea in one of the small teashops to be found in the tree shaded squares in the town. I learnt to ride bareback and enjoyed galloping along the sands. Yes, I was very happy that summer." Her eyes seemed to glaze over as the memories came back.

Carrie smiled to herself, enjoying the mental pictures of RT as a girl. RT's mood suddenly changed as her face adopted a frown.

"As fall set in, I was ordered back to Washington to attend a girls' school. I remember my mother murmuring to my grandmother – "Perhaps they can introduce some femininity into her. My grandmother grimaced and replied, 'Don't be too hard on her Lucy; she's an unusual girl who needs love and attention'. You know, although I could run up and cuddle my darling grandmother, I don't remember ever being hugged or kissed by either of my parents".

Carrie chipped in, "I sort of felt the same way about my mom. She always seemed to want to lead her own life and never had time for me, but I was lucky, my dad was wonderful."

"You were really fortunate then," said RT. "Back in Washington D.C., I didn't last long at the girls' school. I discovered a boys' school across the road and a horrified member of staff found me round the back of the library smoking with a group of the boys. The school was persuaded to give me another chance, but I didn't hesitate to shock them almost immediately – this time it was bootleg liquor I was encouraging two nicely brought up girls to sample."

Carrie was amazed by the formidable woman. She didn't feel shocked but, even though RT was unusual and eccentric, she found it hard to believe all the stories she was hearing.

"After that it was a strict boarding school back in New York State far away from the girls I'd tried to corrupt. I settled down for a time. It was about two years after I was sent to the *exclusive* boarding school that I ran away to go skiing in the Catskills for a long weekend with a friend of my father's. He had come to visit his daughter, and I set out to seduce him. I was only 16 at the time. My parents were very shocked when they caught up with me on the day I absconded, but when I went off again a few months later, the outraged principal decided she'd had enough, and I was expelled. This time I made it much harder for them to catch up with me, I simply disappeared!"

Carrie laughed, "Where did you go?"

"I took off for Paris. It was only when a family friend spotted me on the arm of a notorious Italian Count that they discovered where I was. Needless to say, they dashed over to France and dragged me back to Washington. I was seventeen! However, I wasn't sorry to go home as I was getting very bored with the Count who was becoming more and more possessive. He was very wealthy and took me to all the best restaurants, but as he was three times my age, everybody assumed he was my father, and on several occasions, my grandfather! He hated that."

Carrie ordered more coffee while the old lady went to the 'restroom' and then they settled down to continue their chat.

"Back in the States my parents tried to persuade me to do the social thing with girls of my own age, but after Paris and the high life all the girls of my age seemed so immature, and anyway, the other parents were not too pleased to have their darling daughters mix with someone like me with my scandalous past. So finally, in despair, my father agreed to let me rent my own apartment which, within twelve months, I managed to turn into, what could only be described, as a brothel. You see, I wasn't as sophisticated as I thought I was and when my 'friends' – people I'd met in France and London came to New York, they were only too happy to renew their acquaintance with me and meet up with some of my American girlfriends."

Carrie expressed surprise when RT mentioned the word 'brothel', but RT continued, "I didn't actually set out to run an escort business, it started quite innocently. It was after the first one or two men gave me gifts and pieces of jewellery as a thank you, that I began to encourage others to do the same. Before I knew it, the girls and I were asking for fairly substantial amounts of cash for services. I didn't go out as an escort myself on a general basis as I was very particular about whom I dated, and the men knew and paid accordingly."

Carrie could only open her eyes to these revelations – astonished and surprised by the candidness of this amazing woman. After all, this must have taken place at least fifty years before when women were much more restricted than they had been when Carrie grew up.

"Do go on," suggested Carrie when she noticed what looked like nostalgia creep into the old lady's eyes.

"It was then that I got arrested and did twelve months in a penitentiary," she mused.

"What! You went to jail?"

"Yes. I got caught. One of my girls went out as an escort for a man who turned nasty and beat her up. Badly enough for her to be taken to hospital. I was very naïve in some ways, but you have to remember I was only just nineteen at the time. It never occurred to me that I was doing wrong – accepting money from, what I thought then, were lonely men over here on business. I guessed some of the girls were offering more than just going on a dinner date. Of course, it all came out and hit the headlines of the press. My parents disowned me, naturally. I never saw my father again, but I did make it up with my mother before she died. Listen Honey, I think we'd better be getting home, it's getting late. I'll tell you more about my life another evening."

That night Carrie began writing a journal with all the stories this remarkable woman told her. After a glass or two of wine, RT would sometimes become a little indiscreet and Carrie was able to put two and two together and work out the names of some of the people she had mentioned.

"It was at the penitentiary that I got to know Belle Stone. She was a madam of a very big escort business. Although most of *her* girls only escorted men straight up to the bedroom! She told me where I'd gone wrong and when I came out, she sent me to meet a friend of hers. He was connected to the New York mafia. He was homosexual, gay as your young people now call them and so he wasn't interested in me, but he in turn introduced me to someone else, a man who became my lover for many years until he died in the late seventies."

Carrie was startled when RT told her his name. "But he was famous! Surely, he was connected to the mafia?"

"Oh yes Honey, he was."

"But I remember seeing pictures of him with President Kennedy!"

"Of course. He had access to many high up people, both here in the United States and all over the world. We travelled extensively – to South America, Hong Kong and the Far East. Through him I met Presidents and Princes, Governors, sportsmen and women and, naturally, movie stars. We even once got invited to Buckingham

Palace for a dinner with the Queen. I don't know how he wangled that one. He wasn't particularly interested in going but he knew I really wanted to."

They were having dinner at RT's apartment on the occasion of these disclosures. After the meal RT got up and went into her bedroom where she got her jewellery box out of her personal safe and brought it through to show Carrie.

She began picking out individual pieces and telling Carrie their history, smiling when recalling some of her experiences and frowning over others. Carrie had seen her wearing many of the items during their friendship, but she had never before seen the beautiful bracelet which RT finally pulled out for her inspection.

A dragon made from mixed colours of gold and platinum twisting around RT's wrist when she put it on. Legs and claws stretched along her arm; while the curling tail wrapped itself completely round so that it almost touched the head. But it was the 'fire' the dragon was breathing out that caught Carrie's eyes. On stalks of gold, dozens of small and medium rubies shimmered in the light of the numerous candles on the dining room table. Two large rubies, set in gold springs, quivered and glittered in the dragon's eyes, while all along the ridged back bone were diamonds, beginning with quite large ones from the head and gradually reducing in size down to the tail. In the candlelight the dragon almost appeared to come alive as Carrie stared at it.

"It's beautiful!" gasped Carrie. "Where did it come from?"

"It was passed on to me after a very dear actress friend of mine died. She was given it by a lover who is now very high up in the British

Government, in what they call the House of Lords I believe. He was married at the time, still is as a matter of fact, but back in those days, in the late seventies, it would have really harmed his career if he'd been found out. Things were getting a little too hot as far as he was concerned, and the bracelet was a 'thank you' and 'farewell' gift from him to her. I believe he had it made especially for her when he was on a government trip to Hong Kong. He is a very wealthy man now and was given a title many years ago."

"But how did it come into your possession?" asked Carrie curiously.

"Well, that's another story, but let's just say that, when the actress died *mysteriously*, I was given it as a 'keepsake'. It was really more of a payoff for me to keep my mouth shut. You see, I knew more about her death than I should have done."

"Are you saying she was murdered?" Carrie blurted out, shocked at the thought that one of her favourite actresses had died in any other way than the suicide everybody believed had happened. "Do you know who did it? And why?"

Shadows seemed to cross RT's face, sadness crumpling her old, pale cheeks.

"Oh yes. I knew who arranged it. I was very close to him. Instructions came from very high up. She was becoming a nuisance."

"Did you ever meet the man who gave the bracelet to her?"

"Yes. He once entertained my lover and me in 10 Downing Street, in London, but I'm not saying anything more, I've said more than I should. I've already told you that there are still people out there who could be hurt by what I know."

The women chatted on. Later Carrie suspected that her lover's death wasn't as natural as RT had made out and she was very disturbed by RT's comment that one day someone would probably come for her. It was when RT handed over some papers and told Carrie they were dynamite and should only be handed over to the Democrat Congressman from a State in New England. He was the only one who could deal with them.

"Why can't you give them to him now?" asked Carrie.

"Because he is still in office. I had planned to give them to him on his retirement so that he could take action. At the moment it wouldn't be good for his career. It is just that I am afraid something is going to happen to me. I'm seventy-nine Carrie, I am getting old and tired, and I just have this feeling that my time is limited."

# Chapter 5

It was over dinner one evening while they were sitting in one of their favourite restaurants that Carrie told RT all about her life which had begun in England until she reached the age of four years old. She talked about grade school and high school. About how her mother had left her and her father when Carrie was fifteen and a half.

"I think it was my mom's defection that caused me to fall in love and marry my childhood sweetheart. Life is great now that I've gotten rid of him. He was a thick no-good bastard!"

RT sympathised with her and encouraged her to continue.

"I met him in high school. He'd been feted and admired as captain of the school football team – American of course. He was huge, big, blond and very handsome – and he knew it, but he was mentally thick and very lazy."

The old lady guessed that part of the problem may have been that Carrie was bright and clever.

"I was a cheerleader and most of the girls really envied me when I was metaphorically grabbed by the hero of the 12th grade! William, who was always called Bill - Bill Swallow III. He won a sports scholarship to Berkeley where he proceeded to excel in everything except bookwork. He was on the university football team there and set out to show everyone he could drink beer with the same enthusiasm as he played sports," said Carrie with a sarcastic tone in her voice. "It was drugs that ruined him and got him ignominiously thrown out of Berkeley without getting any exam results."

RT nodded in understanding. After all she had known a great deal about drugs and drug smuggling during her life with her lover.

"When he came back to Southern California, he lied to me and persuaded me that he had been hard done by. He had been the 'good guy' and had taken the rap for someone else. I was dazzled and allowed myself to become engaged and then married to this *oaf*!"

"Some of the most attractive men believe they don't need brains – they think that all they need are their cocks to get them what they want in life!" remarked RT crudely. Carrie nodded her head in agreement, smiling to herself at this remarkable woman.

She went on, explaining that once married, Bill spent his time 'job hunting' in the local bars in Laguna Beach. He had got one job, as a lifeguard on Main Beach, but it didn't last long as he would go on duty having downed at least three cans of Budweiser. The fatal day came when he arrived at the beach too drunk to climb up the ladder to the lookout point to watch the swimmers. He had been sacked on the spot and staggered back to tell his friends in the bar that he was job hunting again. They all happily celebrated the fact.

"And Bill went back to living off his long-suffering wife!" said RT angrily.

"While Bill was away at Berkeley, I did a computer and secretarial course. My father used to say that I would always be able to find work if I had these skills. He was right of course and was absolutely delighted when I got a job with the Laguna Beach Art Festival. What fun it was," Carrie reminisced. "I worked long hours in the summer with the Pageant of the Masters shows every night; the main festival with its many duties; and the Sawdust Festival as well and would often cross over the road to the Sawdust where the scent of marijuana drifted from the back of some of the fake castles selling all sorts of crafts and pictures. Bill liked to come with me on these evenings, but normally he would disappear round the back to join the smokers."

She chatted on to RT, telling her about how she was forced to take on an extra job, working as a cocktail waitress at a local hotel every weekend in order to pay the bills. Bill then began to complain about the men she was supposed to be meeting up with while working in the cocktail bar and so Carrie left both jobs and took on a position as a secretary with an Attorney at Law. It was better paid, but much duller.

"I was twenty-four and we had been married for about four years when I discovered Bill was involved in a drugs racket and threw him out of our home. Unfortunately, I had to sell it in order to give him his share of the assets. However, I was so relieved to get rid of him I threw an 'I got a divorce' party! He moved away to the Lake Tahoe/Reno area."

This really made RT Laugh and say that she wished she'd known Carrie back then, because she certainly would have come.

"I moved back in with my dad and stayed with him until he died in that dreadful accident."

RT lent across the table and squeezed her hand. "I'm so sorry Honey, but at least you got rid of that acid head, Bill Swallow."

"I'm lucky though, I still get on well with my ex-in-laws and go visit them about once a month. His mom is really kind, and his dad said the best thing I ever did was to give Bill the elbow!"

"I'm really glad for you, because you must feel awfully lonely at times. I know what it is like to have no family close by."

Carrie just nodded. At the time she didn't know that these same in-laws would be responsible for the tragedy and disaster that was to occur. On one of her visits, she regaled them with some of the funnier stories about RT, never dreaming they would be passed on to Bill. Even if she had known, it would have made her more careful about what she told them, but she had no idea it would have any significance to Bill and his crooked friends.

# Chapter 6

Having pumped his mother for more information, Bill Swallow made an important phone call. It would net him at least $250,000 if he pulled it off. He had a contract to kill a certain Ms Bushnell in Laguna Beach. He smiled to himself, knowing how upset Carrie would be when she heard her *dear* friend had copped it!

First of all, he had to get her address, but that wasn't difficult, even though she was unlisted in the phone book, Bill still had some good buddies in Laguna, and it didn't take him long to get the information he needed from a former beach bum, now a local mailman.

Next call was to one Mungo, not his real name, he was actually called Padraig O'Reilly, and an Irishman who'd learnt his trade in Northern Ireland. He had managed to escape from Belfast before the authorities caught up with him and put him in the Maze. He was able to enter the United States illegally but once there, he'd offered his services to any rogue who would pay him enough, which is how he became involved with Bill Swallow.

Mungo met up with Bill in Las Vegas when Mungo had been buying a specialist gun for taking people out quietly. Bill walked into the shop while Mungo was doing the deal and got into conversation with him. The two men felt an instant rapport and Bill invited the other man to join him for a drink later at one of the smaller casinos. At a later meeting, Bill learnt that Mungo was also a professional safe breaker as well.

Bill was large, handsome and amusing, whereas Mungo was a small wiry Irishmen with dark hair and piercing blue eyes. On that first evening they simply chatted to each other, each trying to weigh the other up. It wasn't until several months later that Bill asked Mungo to do a job for him. An old lady had been spouting her mouth off to Bill's ex-wife. Unfortunately, some of the things she'd said were detrimental to some very important people and they wanted to shut her up – permanently. Mungo was asked to go and deal with her. The $100,000 offered was enough to make Mungo jump at the chance.

He learnt that Ms Bushnell lived on her own in a house in Laguna Beach. There were certain papers and photographs he had to look for, but more importantly, he had to make the job look like a burglary that went wrong.

"You'll take Joel Hernandez with you, he comes from the area," Bill told him as they discreetly made the arrangements. "I want you to go to the Blue Lagoon Motel on the Coast Highway, just south of Newport Beach. Joel will call you there on Wednesday. Use his vehicle because yours has got Nevada plates and his are false anyway."

They discussed the arrangements for delivering the papers to Bill, and Mungo's escape back to Vegas. The two men slipped away, one to his apartment to get ready for the drive to California and Bill to Caesars Palace Hotel on the Strip to report to his bosses.

# Chapter 7

Joel and Mungo broke into RT's house late on Thursday night. She was preparing for bed and was startled to see them, although in a way she had half expected it for years that sooner or later someone would come after her. What annoyed her was that neither of her handguns was within easy reach. She always kept one hidden in her handbag and the other in a small nightstand beside her bed. She had never envisioned having so little warning of an attack, but when it came it was swift and brutal.

RT put up a good fight for her age, but with two attackers, it didn't last long. Joel grabbed her and Mungo, who had been prepared to use his silenced gun, picked up a heavy brass candlestick from the dining room table in the middle of the room and hit her very hard across her head. The force of the blow thrust her head back with such speed that it broke her neck, and the heart attack, which occurred simultaneously caused her instant death. Her final thoughts were for Carrie and the papers she had given her only that month. She desperately hoped they would not make the link between her and her young friend.

Joel, who was spattered with blood and chips of bone from her skull, just dropped her heartlessly to the floor, where her head lolled uselessly to one side. Wiping the worst of the mess off his clothes, Joel and Mungo began to search the apartment, tossing things around to make it look like a genuine burglary. Joel discovered both of the old lady's guns and pocketed them. Mungo, in the meantime, had specific documents and photographs he had to find, and he began to rummage through RT's desk. He found her safe and proceeded to crack the code fairly quickly.

The Irishman found a few letters and newspaper cuttings that were dated thirty to forty years before, but the item he thought would interest 'the boss' most was a photograph album filled with snaps of many famous people. Among them, two or three in particular, were of a certain famous, now deceased, actress in a rather provocative pose with a very prominent current head of State. Mungo recognised him instantly, because he had been a former Defence Secretary with responsibilities for Northern Ireland and was now Prime Minister of Great Britain! Equally interesting was another photo showing the same politician at what was obviously a clandestine meeting with a man Mungo knew was very high up in the Las Vegas mafia.

What the hell was he doing with him, Mungo speculated to himself? True, there had been rumours in Northern Ireland that the Defence Secretary had not been as honest as he should have been. He had presented himself as a truthful straight-forward man – but stories had surfaced saying he was involved with organised crime and had actually been involved with gun running for the IRA. The whole thing had been put down as rubbish, but Mungo, staring at the photo, began to wonder if he was looking at the evidence – and whether he could make something of it. He wasn't against a spot of blackmail, and the writing on the back certainly implicated the man. Smiling he popped the photo into his pocket, thinking as he did so that he hoped Joel wouldn't miss it.

As he slipped it from the album, he wondered how the hell the old lady had got hold of it. Too late to ask her now! Should he approach the 'Daily Mail, or The Sun' newspapers? He would have to be careful though – it wouldn't do for anyone to connect him with the murder he'd just committed. He thought about making some copies of the other photos, those of the same British politician with the Hollywood actress who had died so mysteriously, but maybe he would go and photocopy everything before handing the papers and pictures over to Bill Swallow, Carrie's former husband.

While Mungo was busy feathering his own nest, Joel was pulling the valuables out of the safe. Jewellery, including the famous 'Dragon's Breath' bracelet went into his pockets. The boss had said to make it look like a burglary and who was he to argue about that! Nobody had said anything about turning in any valuable goods, and Joel reasoned it was his perk for the crime.

Mungo hadn't found any of the papers he was looking for and so they ransacked the apartment further. When they had looked everywhere, Mungo came to the conclusion that the old lady must have destroyed them.

Forty minutes after they had entered the apartment, Mungo and Joel slipped out again – each satisfied with their night's haul.

The two men separated. Joel headed off towards his vehicle parked on a quiet street off the Coast Highway, and Mungo to his car, which he had brought into Laguna Beach against Bill's orders.

Joel made for Laguna Canyon Road and off towards El Toro, while Mungo, taking the same route as far as the freeway, turned north to head out for Nevada to hand over all the papers and photographs to Bill Swallow, after he had found somewhere to copy everything.

# Chapter 8

RT and Carrie had made a date for dinner on the Friday night before going to the Festival to watch the Pageant of the Masters at the open-air theatre. They both loved the extraordinary tableau of local people dressed in costume taking part in recreating works of art. They planned to meet at 5.45pm, have a quick meal at a new Italian restaurant, before heading out to Laguna Canyon for the evening.

When RT didn't show up, Carrie called her on her cell phone but got no answer. She must be on her way and got caught up with all the tourists, thought Carrie. After another fifteen minutes, Carrie was becoming worried that they wouldn't have time to eat and get to the show on time. RT still wasn't answering her phone and so Carrie decided to go and look for her.

Arriving at the house, tucked away on a quiet street, where after knocking she quickly let herself in with the key RT had given her. The appalling mess of RT's things, scattered everywhere, caused Carrie to almost collapse with shock. It was obvious there'd been a burglary and Carrie was terrified the old lady had disturbed them.

There was no sound coming from anywhere. Moving cautiously Carrie began calling for her friend.

"RT, are you here? Where are you? Are you OK? RT….." As she moved further along the passageway leading to RT's main rooms, she had her answer. Her friend was lying where Mungo and Joel had left her. It was obvious the safe had been emptied, the door was open and the picture which had covered it was lying on the floor near RT's shattered head. Carrie felt sick and numb, unable to take in what she was seeing. She didn't know what to do. She was tempted to run, but knew she had to make the call to the authorities. Carrie sank into a chair facing away from the grotesque sight on the floor. She began to gag and had to slow her breathing to stop herself from throwing up.

Trembling, she moved out of the terrible place where her friend lay among smashed possessions, and sat down on the staircase just outside the dining room before dialling 911 to let the local police know. In what seemed like no time at all, she could hear the scream of the sirens. She made her way unsteadily towards the front door, which she had accidently left open, to let them in.

Hardly stopping to speak to her, the crime scene officers raced into the house. Carrie thought detachedly, I wonder why they are in such a hurry. It is too late for them to do anything to help RT.

A woman, dressed in street clothes led her to one of the patrol cars near the front door, where she helped her into the back passenger seat, before joining her there. Carrie vaguely noticed that other uniformed police were ushering pedestrians away and erecting barriers across the road. Thoughts flashed through Carrie's mind – one in particular, was that it was going to cause problems with the festival season.

She turned away from the policewoman and tried to curl up into a foetal position. Great sobs mixed with whimpers and noises that resembled an animal in pain came from her, and then she began to cry. She hadn't cried like this when her father had died, but she had come to love the old lady and felt absolutely desolated by her death.

The policewoman, who turned out to be Barbara Stroud, reached for a box of tissues and let her cry. When Carrie was a little calmer, Barbara explained they were going back to the police station to talk about what had happened. She then read her the Miranda rights and told the driver to head back to the police headquarters.

Once there, she led Carrie into an interview room, got her a cup of coffee, waited until a colleague joined them, and began the questioning.

Carrie told them how she was waiting for RT at the restaurant, and when she hadn't responded to her cell phone call, she had decided to go round to her house.

"You said you let yourself in. Did you have a key?"

"Yes, RT gave me a set in case she got sick. Then I could get in if she needed me to.".

Barbara thought she was about to cry again, but Carrie took a deep breath and sitting upright in a rigid fashion, she told the policewoman what she had seen.

The questioning went on and on. They went over Carrie's evidence about her movements over the past twenty-four hours exhaustively. At one point someone came in with some sandwiches, but Carrie was too distraught to touch them.

"I wish I hadn't changed the date! We were originally going to the Pageant on Thursday night, but one of my friends was holding a wedding shower on that evening and so we changed the tickets. If I hadn't, she might still be alive."

"Why do you say that? Right now, we don't know when she died."

"She was so cold!" Carrie shuddered as she said it.

"How do you know? Did you touch her?"

"Just her hand. She was just lying there. I didn't know if she was still alive. But she was so cold!" repeated Carrie.

Later it was confirmed by the coroner who'd done the autopsy that Ms RT Bushnell died at least twenty hours before she'd been found.

"You went to the wedding shower. Tell me about it."

"It was at my friend Olivia's house in Mission Viejo. There were a big group of girls, about twenty of us. I knew it was going to be a late night and so I had taken overnight gear with me. Olivia had asked me to stay over, then I could join in the wine and champagne celebrations. Most of the other girls were getting their husbands or boyfriends to pick them up. Three of them shared a cab, but I don't have either a husband or local boyfriend, so it was easier to stay at Olivia's".

"I need names and addresses so I can verify this."

"After the others left, Olivia and I sat up and talked until about 2.30 in the morning. I know it was that late because we both commented on how late it was, and we both had to work in the morning."

The note taking went on. At one point the policewoman left her colleague to continue the questions. When she came back, she said,

"Well, if your alibis stand up, it looks as though you are in the clear because you couldn't have killed her."

Carrie was totally shocked at the suggestion that she might have murdered her friend.

"Me? Kill RT? But I wouldn't….. She was my friend. I loved her like a mother," and with the horror of the whole thing, Carrie fainted. The police personnel on the other side of the table were not quick enough to catch her as she hit the hard floor.

"Try and get her friend Olivia Richards on her cell phone, you've got the number there in the notes. Then get the paramedics here to take Mrs Swallow to the emergency room at the hospital. See if Ms Richards can meet us there. We can talk to her before she and Mrs Swallow have a chance to confirm each other's story. Ms Richards can take her home if the hospital doesn't want to keep her in."

The police interviewed each of the women separately and were satisfied they were telling the truth, and so about 5.45 in the morning the friends left, and Olivia took Carrie to her own home. She tried to persuade Carrie to eat or drink something, but Carrie just shook her head. Olivia waited until she was in her bed and quietly left.

# Chapter 9

Next morning, Carrie got up early and forced herself to drink a strong cup of coffee. She couldn't face anything else with the shocking memories of the brutal murder. Then she began doing what she normally did. Turning on her lawn sprinklers and topping up the hummingbird feeders – anything to take her mind off the horrors of the previous evening.

Olivia called to see how she was and was surprised when Carrie said she was going into work.

"I have to do something. If I sit here all day I shall just cry".

"If you feel bad, I'll come and get you."

"No, I'll be fine", replied her friend – lying.

It was eight months later when a man, a stranger to her came into the bank and asked to let him into his safe deposit box. That was the beginning of what was about to happen to her. At this moment her life changed forever. She knew she had looked into the killer's eyes!

Flo took one look and asked what was wrong. Carrie wasn't ready to talk about the violence in the safe deposit room, and everyone knew about the brutal murder of her friend some 8 months before.

"Sorry, just felt a little faint – wrong time of the month. I'll go into the staff room for a few minutes – I'm sure I will be OK shortly"

Flo looked very concerned and suggested she should go home.

"We are not likely to be busy today, and in any case, if we are the customers will have to wait!"

Carrie went off to the staff room, thankful it was empty and quiet as it wasn't time for the first lot of staff to come through for lunch.

She waited until she stopped trembling before returning to her desk, her mind a jumble of thoughts. For the rest of the day, she allowed the other girls to do the jumping up and down and let people into their boxes. She couldn't face going back into the vault, at least not that day.

She was still in a state of shock when she left at 5.30 and climbed into her red Mustang to drive home. She didn't notice another car pull away and follow her out of the shopping area and on to the freeway. It was only when she turned off the Coast Highway in South Laguna and on to the little road that led to her house, that she was surprised to see the same vehicle, which had been following her down the freeway, was still behind her when she pulled onto her driveway.

Her mind and body froze. What if it was somebody to do with the murder? Now they know where I live. Dear God, what can I do? she cried out in anguish.

The car drove on slowly past the bottom of the road, and Carrie heaved a sigh of relief while she pulled her car into the garage and pressed the button to close the door.

"I'm just getting paranoid for no reason at all", speaking out loud as she let herself into her tiny hall. Usually, Carrie would go over to open the patio windows, but she was still too nervous to do that. In her fridge there was a bottle of white wine, which she opened before sitting down to think about what she should do.

# Chapter 10

As a friend of RT, she had been intensively interviewed by the police, but as they considered the death was part of a burglary, and her statements were confirmed by a number of people, they had merely questioned her and asked her to make herself available for the inquest.

Carrie had been very touched when a Will had been found in RT's apartment leaving her RT's entire estate, which included the money in RT's savings accounts, plus her jewellery. The money was safe, but all her jewellery had disappeared when the apartment was ransacked during the robbery and murder and, until today, nobody knew where the valuable items, including the Dragon's Breath bracelet, had gone, except Carrie – and the murderer – which made her very vulnerable.

When Carrie had been interviewed by the police, she did not show them the diaries, or tell them about RT's colourful life, because she didn't think it had anything to do with what seemed to be a common break in and burglary. Now she began to wonder.

As she sat in her sitting room with the light rapidly fading, she heard a car drive up and stop outside. Carrie was about to switch on the light beside her chair, when she stiffened and sat bolt upright.

Someone was outside. She waited for the front doorbell to ring, but nothing happened. She sat completely still - unable to move. Terrified, she felt and sensed, rather than saw, someone peering through the window. The young woman pressed her body back in the chair, relieved that it was a big antique winged armchair which hid her from view, and prayed they wouldn't see her, but just go away. She didn't even dare to breathe, in case they should hear her - and then, as suddenly, as it had arrived, the presence seemed to disappear. With relief, she heard the car start up again, turn around and head back down to the Coast Highway.

Carrie sat still and tense in her chair for at least another 10 minutes, frantically trying to decide what to do next. She never even considered calling the police. RT had instilled the idea into her that somehow the police authorities were behind some of the bizarre happenings in RT's life.

"I was more likely to get locked up, than helped out", RT once said when Carrie questioned her about why she hadn't gone to the police over her actress friend's death.

"No" she added, "whatever happens to me - stay clear of the police. Tell them as little as possible - and *don't* volunteer any information!"

Now when Carrie thought about the police, she was afraid. But what could she do? Who could she turn to?

"I've got to get away - far away! But where?" She murmured, I could go and visit my mother - but would that put her in danger? No, I'd be better leaving the States and going somewhere else". She thought about Australia, her mother's home country - but then rejected it. She hadn't really been on good terms with her mother since she walked out on Carrie and her father when Carrie was fifteen and a half. No, Abby Merchant or, as she was now Mrs Abigail Carruthers, would not want her daughter interfering in any way in her life.

No, thought Carrie, mum's family are out. I'll have to go to England. But where in England? The only place she could think of was to visit her eccentric godmother. She glanced at the clock and murmured; it will be the middle of the night in England right now - I'll have to wait to call her when I get over there.

Decision made; Carrie considered her next step. She had two passports locked up in her safe deposit box at the bank, one English in the name of Caroline Merchant and the other, American, Carrie Swallow, so she knew she would have to go into work in the morning in order to collect them. In fact, it be better to act normally, in case someone was watching her.

Other thoughts raced through her mind – money; airline tickets; how was she going to get to the airport. She knew she couldn't fly straight out of California to England. Somehow, she needed to conceal her departure.

When she got to work, she decided she would take out sufficient money to pay cash for a while but leave enough so that her box remained valid at the bank.

And how am I going to get away and get to the airport? she thought worriedly while sitting in what was now pitch darkness. And what will I do about my house and my car?

Carrie then remembered her close friend Olivia Richards who was a real estate broker. I'm sure she'll help me, she said out loud to herself.

Before Carrie turned on any lights, she carefully made her way over to her windows and closed the drapes. Switching on one low lamp she picked up her handheld phone to call her friend. It took ages for Olivia to answer, and Carrie began to worry that her friend was out.

"Hi. Olivia Richards here. How may I help you?"

"Olivia. It's me - Carrie. I *really* need your help. Can you come over? *Now?*"

"Carrie, you sound awful! What's the problem?"

"I can't talk on the phone. *Please, please can you come now*" she said desperately.

"Yes sure. I'm just closing a sale on a house in Dana point. We are nearly done. I could be with you in – say – three quarters of an hour?"

"Thanks Olivia. You don't know how relieved I am. Look - when you get here the house will look dark as though no one's at home. Instead of ringing the bell can you just knock three times on the front door - that way, I'll know it's you".

"Wow! Carrie, that sounds really scary! I'll hurry it up here and get to you as soon as possible".

"Thanks Olivia" repeated Carrie - but Olivia was already gone.

Carrie decided to go into a small travel agency in Laguna Niguel to buy her tickets to travel back to England. She didn't know this travel agency and so she felt fairly safe. She still had her American credit cards and decided to use two of these. She knew it was a bit dodgy, but she felt she had to take the risk anyway. The same cards would be left behind locked in her safe deposit box. She would go into the travel agents and book two separate tickets, one for her flight from Newport Beach to Atlanta GA, and the other for the flight from Atlanta to London, using a different card for each flight.

Carrie considered what she should take with her and decided as little as possible. She would put as much as she possibly could into a bag that would go into the overhead locker on the plane. She could always buy anything else she needed when she got to her godmother's house. By only taking one bag, she wouldn't need to check in any luggage for the onward flight to London. Carrie was relieved she could go from Newport Beach because it was only a 20-minute drive from where she worked and at this time, she had no idea whether Olivia would be able to drive her to catch the 12:30 flight, and if she couldn't Carrie was not sure what she should do. Fortunately, when she asked Olivia, she said she'd be happy to help her

That done she pondered about her car which was left in the car park surrounding the bank. She decided she would ask Chuck at her friendly service station, where she took her beloved vehicle for its regular checks to come and collect it and then sell it for her. I can leave the keys with a security guard and tell him it's being picked up to check out the muffler. I'll have to remember to call it an exhaust pipe when I get to England, she thought smiling to herself.

Looking in her address book she found Chuck's telephone number and called him next. He was very surprised at her request because he knew she treated her car like it was her baby. Explaining she needed to go and visit her mother who was very sick, and she didn't know how long it would be before she was back and so he agreed to do as asked.

"One thing though Chuck", she added "please don't let on at the bank that I'm going away - just go along with the story that I'm getting my car serviced – *please*".

"Sure Carrie. Whatever you say. But what should I do with the money when I've sold the car for you? Shall I just send you a cheque, or deposit it in your bank account?"

"My bank account please. I'll give you my account number at the bank please just send the cheque to the bank and tell them to deposit it in my account".

"Sure, thing Carrie but it still seems strange. You don't want me to keep the car for you for when you return?"

"No. No just sell it for me please. Bye Chuck, I'll call you sometime and let you know what's happening"

"Bye Carrie, hope your mom gets better real soon".

Carrie began sorting out the things needed to be taken with her. Some clothes but not too many. She had already decided she didn't want to be burdened with too much luggage, and besides, anything she was taking would have to be put into Olivia's car tonight. She certainly didn't dare transfer anything in daylight in the middle of a busy car park.

Startled some 10 minutes later, when there was a knock on the door, followed by two more. Carrie froze in terror again - and then remembered she had told Olivia to use this method for letting her know when she'd arrived. Carrie recovered her composure but before opening the door she checked through the little spy hole in the middle of the front door to make absolutely sure it was Olivia.

"Hi, come on in. Boy, am I glad to see you!" She cried out. almost dragging her friend in.

"Hey, what's with the dark in here? I can't see where I'm going!"

"Never mind come on through to the kitchen and I'll turn on some lights. What have you got with you? It smells like pizza".

"It is pizza. I haven't had time to eat since breakfast this morning and I'm starving! I just stopped off at that pizza place on the Coast Highway and got us a pepperoni pizza. You've got wine or beer here, haven't you?

Carrie nodded, "I guess I'm hungry too, and yes, I've got some wine. What is it to be? Red? White?"

"Red please. Something 'full bodied'".

Carrie went over and pulled a bottle out of her wine rack on one of the kitchen counters.

"My wine cellar" as she laughingly called it. "How's this? A nice Paul Masson from the Napa Valley.

"Great", replied Olivia as she expertly divided the pizza between two plates.

"We will eat inside, if you don't mind Olivia. I'm a little afraid to go out back."

"It's OK, of course. Now - tell me what's wrong. You sounded in one hell of a state when you called me."

"Did your sale go through OK?"

"Come on Carrie don't change the subject. What's wrong?"

"I don't know where to start."

"Well, you were fine last night when I spoke to you - telling me all about your vacation up at June Lake. You said it was great to be up in the mountains and you sounded so happy. But you're completely different today, and so something must have happened between 9:00 last night and now."

"Yes. Something has happened. Olivia, do you remember my friend RT?"

"Yes, of course. Funny old lady! Always thought she was a bit odd, but she's dead, isn't she? Wasn't she murdered about eight months back? She had a break-in in her apartment while she was at home, and she was killed, and they took off with all her valuables? They haven't found the bastard who did it yet, have they?"

Carrie shook her head, and Olivia could see tears well up in her eyes.

"Yes, she was - and I think I know who did it."

"*You - what*?" exclaimed Olivia.

"A man came into the bank today. I checked his name on the details we had on file after he left. His name on his card said Joel Hernandez. Mexican, it sounds, although he didn't look or sound very Mexican. Anyway, he came in and got out his safe deposit box, which he dropped. Everything fell out all over the floor – *and Olivia*, a bracelet owned by RT fell out of the box! When I saw it, I nearly cried out that it was mine! He knew I recognised it and Olivia; he threatened to kill me if I told anyone what I saw!"

"Oh God, Carrie. Why are you telling me?"

"I've got to tell someone because I'm going to run away!"

"Where? Where are you going?"

"It's best I don't tell you right now. It's just this, can you rent out this house for me? I don't know for how long - six months - maybe a year? Until I hear the police have caught this man anyway."

"Don't you think you ought to call the police right now and tell them what you know?"

"No. I don't. RT always told me not to tell the police anything."

"But Carrie, how are they going to catch the man if you don't give them his name?"

"You're right, of course. But I won't call them from here. I'll wait until I get where I'm going".

"OK, Carrie. I guess you really *are* scared. About your house - of course I can rent it out for you - but I need to know where you're going so I can correspond with you over the details."

"No. I'll sign everything now. I'm sure you've got all the forms in that bulging briefcase of yours. I *trust* you, Olivia. Rent it out for me and send the monthly payments to my bank. Here - I've written down the account number and so on."

"Well, we can do it that way, but what about your stuff here?"

"Can you arrange to get it packed up and put into storage for me? Take the payments out of my account. I'll sign a direct debit for you for $1000 per month. That should cover the storage costs and your management fee."

"Hey Carrie - I don't want any money for myself!!

"Yes, you must! *Please* Olivia. If I know you're being paid, then I'll be more comfortable about leaving all this mess for you to sort out. Oh, one other thing - can you get a 'Letting' board up as soon as possible? If that Joel Hernandez comes by again - he'll know I've gone and hopefully will leave me alone."

"Carrie, don't you think you *should* call the cops?" Repeated Olivia.

"No. As I told you, RT stressed again and again not to involve the cops. Whoever was involved with her death could go up as high as the president!"

"Oh, come on, Carrie! Do you really believe the ramblings of an old woman?"

"Surprisingly, I do. There were a couple of occasions when she had very large amounts of cash hidden in her apartment. She'd always said she was had to be careful with her money - and yet on one occasion she suddenly produced about $150,000 from cushions on her Ottoman and from shoeboxes. I persuaded her to put the money into an account in the bank. When I asked her where all this money had come from, she muttered darkly about a 'payoff' - and then, not three weeks later, she produced another $35,000 from the same places! I've asked myself time and time again where it came from, and I just don't know the answer! I'm beginning to think though, that her murder was more than a burglary. Were they looking for something special? Maybe papers or letters that could incriminate some well-known person? Was the cash she was getting a payoff as she said – or was she blackmailing someone? I just don't have an answer to the question."

"So, *you* are running away?"

"Yes. I'm terrified, Olivia. It was my bad luck I happened to take Mr Hernandez into the vault and saw the 'Dragon's Breath' bracelet."

"OK. I must trust you - time is getting on - we'd better get the paperwork out of the way."

"One other thing, Olivia, I have arranged for my car to be picked up, ostensibly for servicing - but actually for sale. Someone will be coming to collect it from the car park by the bank. Could you possibly take my bag with you tonight? I'm only taking an overnight bag with me. Can you pick me up tomorrow at about 11:00 am from the back entrance of the May Company department store and take me to the airport?"

"I'll come to the bank if you like."

"No. I've thought about it. When I go for a coffee break tomorrow, I'll tell the girls I've got to run over to the store to buy a gift for someone's birthday. I'll go in through the main entrance and then quickly make my way over to the back entrance facing onto the area where the Mexican restaurant is. Then, if anyone is watching me, hopefully they'll wait for me to come back out the same way."

"Aren't you going to tell your boss you're quitting?"

"No. *You* are. After you've taken me to the airport and I'm on the plane, please can you just phone and say I've gone?"

"Well, of course I can - but don't you think it's a bit hard on them?"

"But what else can I do? I'm terrified I'll be killed like RT was. You do understand, don't you? Tell them I'll be back. Point out I'm leaving my accounts open and keeping my safe deposit box. Oh, and please could you say how very, very sorry I am to be letting them down."

"Yes - I'll do all that for you, my friend. Now, come on, we need to get your bags packed, etc. I'm afraid I haven't any time to do a full inventory for you - I'm sorry."

"I was going to call a removal company to come and collect my stuff."

"Don't worry about that, I know a company in San Juan Capistrano. I'll sort it for you. Hey, and I'll take all your personal stuff. I've plenty of room in my spare bedroom. The closet and drawers are all empty, so I can put things in there.”

“Thank you. I don’t know how long I’m going to be away for, so you may have them in your house for some time. I want you to take the wine and other liquor I’ve got here, plus any food you can use. The freezer is full - please help yourself.”

“I will, Carrie, I will – but I am sure going to miss you.”

The two friends gave each other a warm hug and then got on with the things they needed to do before Carrie quit her home.

# Chapter 11

After Olivia left with Carrie's suitcases in her car, Carrie wandered round her much-loved home with tears running down her face. She had never for one moment imagined leaving it - at least not as a single woman without a family.

She was still in shock as she lay down on her bed for the last time for the foreseeable future. She was very tired, but sleep wouldn't come. Every tiny sound jerked her into a sitting up position. Once, the outside security lights came on in her back tard and she crept out of bed to peer out, only to find a family of skunks nosing around.

I shan't see you for a while, she murmured into the darkness. I only hope the next people put out dog biscuits and things for you to enjoy. The thought of leaving her friends and her work, Southern California, and the climate she revelled in for the cold, wetter climate of Great Britain, caused the tears to start again.

"It's so unfair! I was only being kind to an old lady! Why should I be involved in this mess?" But she knew she had willingly invited the confidences RT had told her.

"Tomorrow", she said to herself, "I'll get to the bank early and park my car where I told Chuck I would leave it. Then I'll get my passport and things out of my safe deposit box and close out my regular account - I think I've got about $25,000 in it, but I'll leave the one-year deposit account, and that will cover the terms for holding the box. After that, I'll open the department as per normal. At around 10:30, I'll tell the girls I'm going to run over to May company to buy a birthday gift instead of taking my coffee break - and hopefully, Olivia will be where I asked her to be, and I'll simply just vanish!"

At 5:30 am Carrie decided to forget trying to sleep and got up and automatically made up her bed, pulling up the bright Mexican bedspread, and piling nearly a dozen multi coloured cushions on top - together with some old dolls dressed in colourful costumes, which she propped up against the cushions. Walking into her bathroom, she turned on a hot shower, relieved that she had survived the night. When the security lights had come on during the night, she thought it was Joel Hernandez coming to kill her. Somehow, with her life falling apart around her, she had been less terrified then than when the car had stopped outside the evening before.

Then, Carrie made her way into the kitchen. Coffee percolator switched on and juice poured ready to drink, together with the slice of toast she'd made, she went out into the garden one last time to fill the hummingbird's container. Watching the little birds come buzzing in, Carrie walked round her oasis of calm, filled with the scent and colour of the flowers and shrubs she had so carefully planted and tended. She stopped to breathe deeply at the gardenia in the flower bed closest to the corner where her bedroom jutted out beside her kitchen. She'd planted it there so the beautiful scent could invade her windows. Then on to the lemon and orange trees, which carried both flowers and fruit at the same time.

Some of the lemons were ripening, she thought - I was looking forward to picking them to have with a vodka and tonic when I sit out here in the dusk, while listening to the sound of the crickets and watching the sun disappear, as it seemed to do so quickly into the Pacific Ocean. I shall miss you all so much, and her heart felt like breaking.

Carrie returned to her kitchen, where she drank the juice and coffee but threw the toast into the bin, knowing she couldn't eat it. She dressed for work in her bank uniform, picked up her large handbag in which she had placed a light pair of jeans and an inconspicuous T-shirt to change into, along with trainers, a baseball cap, and dark glasses. She added a scrunchy for her hair. Her uniform would go into a May Co bag, which was also hidden in her handbag, and then she would make her way through the store and out the back entrance, where Olivia would be waiting

At 7:45 am, Carrie nervously opened her front door and stepped out. She glanced up and down the road, but nothing struck her as being unusual. Carrie opened the garage door, and after throwing her things into her car, she dropped the soft top and drove away. The frown on her face eased as she thought to herself, I got through the night, and in less than six hours - God willing - I'll be on a plane heading towards Atlanta and then Europe.

Carrie hadn't been happy she couldn't get a direct flight to London from Newport Beach, and she only had a two-hour stopover in Atlanta, and so she had to be relieved by that. That would give her time to get from the internal flight terminal to the international one. Upon consideration, Carrie decided it was probably better to stop down within the US in order to put anyone following her to lose track

The road dipped deeply down from the outside of her house to the Coast Highway. Carrie drove slowly, looking out towards the Pacific Ocean. She could just see the dull smudge of Catalina Island on the horizon. Memories flooded back to the time when her father had hired a small Cessna from the little airport at San Juan Capistrano just before it was closed down for security reasons. The two of them had flown over to the island for breakfast - landing on the runway high above the town. Her father pointed out the Buffalo grazing on the hillside and told the story of how they'd come to be on the island.

"They were making a film", he'd said, "they needed Buffalo in it, but when the film was over, they couldn't be bothered to take them back to the mainland, and the buffalo established themselves as a herd."

It was around this time that Carrie decided she wanted to learn to fly. Her father let her handle the controls and she learnt how to fly 'straight and level', how to bank the plane into a turn, and how to 'enter the pattern'. He never allowed her to actually land the plane, but she'd gone through the procedures so many times in her head that, not long after her 16th birthday, she was off on her initial solo flight. It had been really scary when the instructor jumped out of the plane and just said - "Off you go then - I'll wait down here for you."

It had been harder than she realised. It was OK with her calm and confident instructor sitting next to her, but it was another thing to be up in the air on her own.

Speaking aloud to herself, she said, "Help! I can't just pull over and think about it – I've got to get this thing down".

The runway looked awfully small, and in her slight panic, she knew she was coming in a bit low, so taking a deep breath, she added power, pulled back on the steering column, and went around again. This time she landed safely, although a bit hard, making the small plane bounce a couple of times.

"Whew", she said as her instructor ran over, "that was scary!"

"Well done, Carrie. You've now completed your first solo; you can only go on with your flying career".

When Carrie landed, they had cut off part of the back of her favourite shirt to hang as a trophy in the clubhouse. But she hadn't minded because she'd been so exhilarated.

Back to reality, she was suddenly aware of reaching the busy main highway, heading south toward San Diego and north towards Los Angeles, via the Coast Highway. She saw people driving to work and mothers dropping their kids off at school.

"Can I bear to leave this all behind?" She wondered. "It will be hard, so hard, but what else can I do at the moment?"

Carrie turned south on the Coast Highway, and then a mile or so further on she turned left to travel up Crown Valley Parkway towards the San Diego freeway.

As she drove, she marvelled yet again at how fast the place was changing. When she and her family moved out from England in 1971, she was four years old and there were a few housing developments up in the hills but now it was wall to wall houses and apartments. She preferred the old way.

Reaching the centre of Laguna Niguel, Carrie turned into the car park in front of the travel agency. The young woman behind the counter seemed half asleep, but then it was still early, and maybe she'd had a very late night out partying! Carrie pulled out her two credit cards and asked the woman to make up two separate tickets, one for the flight from Newport Beach to Atlanta and a separate one for the flight between Atlanta and London. The woman seemed a bit surprised but did as she was asked. Carrie had handed her English passport in the name of Caroline Jane Merchant over to the young woman, who fortunately didn't notice the name on the credit card was different from that on the passport, and she made out the tickets in Carrie's maiden name. Carrie felt that she was at least making some headway.

That job completed and the tickets safely tucked away in her purse, Carry turned north on the freeway and joined the mass of cars and trucks heading towards the Los Angeles basin and all the towns and cities in between. She didn't have to go too far, just a few miles before she got off again and made her way towards Laguna Hills and the bank where she worked.

Car parked; she entered the bank. The security guard called out a cheerful 'good morning' and Flo, her immediate subordinate in the Safe Deposit Department and who arrived soon after, enquired about her health.

"Are you OK today? I was worried about you because it isn't like you to get sick."

"I'm fine, thanks. I'll be OK. Oh - and by the way, Flo, I'm just nipping out at break time - I've got to pick up a gift for my friend's birthday. If I'm a bit longer - cover for me, will you please?"

"Sure, no problem. Hey, I understand we're getting Sally over here today - want me to start the basic training for you?"

"Please, if you wouldn't mind. I've got a couple of personal things to do. I want to go into my box, and I need to take some money out of my account."

Carrie went into the box filled with RT's documents and journals, incriminating photos, and letters kept by the old lady over many years. She was relieved to find everything still intact. Locking it back up again, she planned to leave that key in her own box. She went across the large safe deposit box room, unlocked her own box, and dropped the key into it. She took out her passbooks for her different accounts and noticed they hadn't been updated for a while. 'Too busy', she told herself. Then she removed her passports, both her American and British ones. Later, she wondered why she had taken her American passport along with her, as she wasn't going to need it. But maybe when she came back to America, it would be useful, and so she put both of them in her jacket pocket. She had decided to leave her bits and pieces of jewellery in the box along with the diaries in which she had recorded the information gleaned from RT. Before closing the box, Carrie took out her cell phone, switched it off, and dropped it in amongst the other things, including her California driving licence, hoping it wouldn't be necessary to use her cell phone to call Olivia before they met at the back door of the store. I can't be burdened with any more than I need, she said to herself, and anyway, I'm afraid with modern technology, they or whoever, might be able to trace where I've gone to.

One of her colleagues, Jolene, was currently acting as a teller, and she updated her passbooks. Carrie was surprised that they hadn't had the interest added for over six months.

She'd already worked out what to say to Jolene.

"Hi Jolene, I need to take $20,000 out of this account, please – in cash. I've found a cabin up in the Sierra Nevada mountains, near Mammoth Lakes, and I need to money to put down to buy it".

"Shall I prepare a cashier's cheque for you?"

"No, thank you. The present owner says they are a bit off the beaten track and would prefer cash".

Jolene said, "OK. Just take care and don't get mugged! $20,000 is a lot of money".

"No worries, I shan't have it on me for long".

"Would you like me to put it into an envelope for you?".

"Thanks, Jolene, yes please, and I promise to take care of it!" Carrie replied, attempting to put a laugh into her voice.

Back at her desk, she dropped the envelope containing the money into her purse. She took a quick glance at her passports. Both up to date – although she wasn't planning to use the American one, at least now. She was relieved she had remembered to book her ticket in her maiden name, which was the one in her English passport. She'd never gotten round to changing it after she married Bill, because they'd never been out of the country. Perhaps if they had, she would have made the effort to get the name changed - but as it was, she'd just left it sitting in her safe deposit box.

Carrie knew there wasn't a problem flying between Newport Beach and Atlanta because she wouldn't need a passport for that leg, and on the leg between Atlanta and London, she would be able to show her English passport, which matched the name on the ticket.

Money and passports, securely tucked away, she was ready to go through the pretence of doing a full day's work.

Carrie watched the clock. It seemed to move so slowly. 10.30 finally arrived, and Carrie slipped off for her coffee break. She went out through the main entrance and missed seeing someone messing around underneath her car. The man under her car was wearing mechanics' overalls, and so nobody took any notice of him. Joel Hernandez, who was with the man beneath the car, did see her, though, and followed her across the parking lot into the front entrance of the department store.

Following her, but not too closely in case she should turn around and recognise him, he watched Carrie go up to the first floor and then into the ladies' powder room. Mr Hernandez felt a bit conspicuous standing around in the lingerie department, and he began to move away, especially when he saw some security men looking at him curiously. But he didn't go too far because he didn't want to miss seeing her come out again. While he waited, he hoped his colleague had finished doing the job on Carrie's car - it would never do for her to see what little surprise they had ready for her!

Carrie had carefully chosen this particular area of the store and was now, unknown to her watcher, rapidly changing out of her bank uniform and into the jeans and T-shirt she concealed in her bag, along with a casual blazer. A pair of trainers replaced her plain navy leather, high-heeled work shoes. She swiftly pulled her hair back into a ponytail, pulled on a baseball cap, covered her eyes with a large pair of sunglasses, and then added a bright lipstick in place of the pale pink she usually wore. She put all her work clothes, including her shoes and bag, into the May Company shopping bag she'd brought with her, and made her way back out into the main shopping area.

The Carrie who came out of the ladies' powder room looked completely different from the one who'd gone in. She walked out in a leisurely fashion, checking out underwear, looking like a woman engrossed in shopping and not as a fugitive fleeing for her life. Joel Hernandez noticed a woman come out of the ladies' room and thought to himself - typical vain Californian woman! Fancy wearing dark glasses in a department store, and he didn't give her another thought as she idly wandered through the shop looking at first one thing and then another, before taking the elevator down to the ground floor and out through the back entrance.

Olivia was also surprised and almost refused to let her friend get into her car. It was only when Carrie spoke that Olivia quickly opened the passenger door and said, "Quick - come on, let's go!"

They were within two minutes of getting onto the freeway when an enormous explosion occurred in the car park by the bank. Carrie had no idea that it had been her car that was blown up, along with poor Chuck inside it. As they sped away, Carrie dropped the visor so she could watch in the mirror to see if anyone was following them

"What a weirdo!" The girl in the store said to her friend after she'd finished serving a customer,"

"Yeah - I saw him standing around staring in this direction. Looked like he was following someone. We'd better just put a call down to security and get them to watch out for him. You know it's strange, I thought I saw someone of that description going to the ladies changing room over there - but I never saw her come out. I must have been busy," she said as she shrugged her shoulders while her friend dialled the number of the head of security.

As it happened, the watcher suddenly became the watched. Security got him on their cameras and followed him through the store. He was definitely not a shopper - not the way he was looking up and down the aisles between the goods on offer. When he left the store, he was oblivious to the fact that the head of security followed him out and almost over to where his associate was standing near Carrie's red Mustang.

Mungo Fisher was wiping his hands on a cloth or paper towel when he was joined by Joel. They had a brief conversation and then climbed into a silver-grey Buick. The head of security noted down the number plate and returned to his office. There he put a call through his to his wife, who worked at the local police department. She agreed with him it was a bit strange and offered to run the car number through her computer to see what came up.

"I'll let you know later", she said. But they were too late, Joel and Mungo had already slipped to the back of the parking lot and parked almost alongside a container truck. They got out of Mungo's car and headed towards Joel's, which was parked right by the truck. They had foreseen that they might have been watched and had left Joel's car hidden behind the truck. They didn't care how quickly the Buick was found because it had false plates on it and could not be traced back to them, as the head of security's wife discovered when checking car registrations.

"Where the hell did, she go?", he said reporting to Mungo as they headed for the freeway and eventually back to Los Angeles.

"I followed her up to the 3rd floor and watched her go into the changing rooms, but she didn't come out. I don't know how she did it, she just disappeared."

"Perhaps she changed – in the changing room", laughed Mungo. "Well, she's bound to come back to collect her car at some point and when she switches on the engine she's in for one hell of a shock".

They were just pulling away when there was a huge explosion and a big cloud of smoke in the parking lot.

"That'll be the end of her! Hey Joel, put your foot down and get the hell out of here. The cops will be swarming all over the place shortly".

Back in Olivia's car, also heading north, but about 20 minutes ahead of the murderers, Olivia said -

"Wow, Carrie! You look so different! I haven't seen you with a ponytail in years."

"Well, I hope I fooled anyone who might have been watching. Just to change the subject did you get a 'To let' board up on my house yet?"

"No. I thought I'd leave it until I get it cleared, and then I'll put the board up - probably tomorrow. I'm going to go back there after I've left you at the airport to clear your fridge out, etc. What do you want me to do about your mail?"

"Can you have it forwarded to your address, please?"

"No problem. I'll open up the ones that look like bills and pay them for you - anything personal, I'll just hang on to it until you give me a forwarding address."

"Thanks, Olivia. You're a *great* friend!"

It wasn't long before they turned off the freeway and onto the road to the airport. Carrie wouldn't allow her friend to come into the building with her, and so they said goodbye at the entrance to departures. They hugged each other, and both women walked away with tears in their eyes. Olivia was hoping the murderer of RT would be caught quickly so her friend could come back, and Carrie was heading for an unknown future. Carrie also felt worried and guilty that she had involved Olivia in her plight, and she hoped the thugs would leave her friend alone.

As Olivia drove away, Carrie hurried into the main departure area and headed for the Delta Airlines departure desk.

Boarding pass in hand, she picked up her cabin bag and made her way through to the departure lounge to collapse on a seat facing the door through which she'd come. In that way, she could watch out for anyone who might be looking for her.

By the time the flight was called, Carrie had begun to relax a little. Nobody seemed interested in her, but she was relieved when she got on the plane and found she was sitting on her own. The aircraft wasn't full, and Carrie sat in the window seat watching Newport Beach and California slide away from beneath her.

"Would you like something to drink?" Carry glanced up, startled, because she had been so deeply into her own thoughts.

"Sorry?" She said."

"Would you care for something to drink?" repeated the stewardess, with a smile on her face.

"Yes. Yes, please, I'll have a Bloody Mary."

"With ice?"

"Yes, thank you."

The stewardess put down a little bag of peanuts, followed by a miniature bottle of vodka and a can of Bloody Mary mix.

"Thank you," repeated Carrie.

Carrie finished her drink and dozed off - tiredness setting in. For the moment, she felt safe. It was only when the plane landed in Atlanta that she began to feel panicky again.

What if they find out where I'm going? What if they are waiting for me at the airport in Atlanta? What if they have found Olivia? Her conscious mind told her nobody could know where she was. 'Carrie Swallow had disappeared - it was Caroline Merchant arriving in Atlanta. Her subconscious mind reminded her that she'd got two whole hours to make her way across to the international flights terminal, and she had to keep alert.

Before she left the internal flights terminal, Carrie decided to change some of her money from dollars into pounds. She thought she'd wait to change more of it when she got to the international terminal. She didn't want people questioning why she was changing so much money at one time. She was prepared for curiosity and was ready to explain that she was eventually off to move into a new apartment in England and needed to pay for her accommodation in pounds sterling. However, nobody seemed interested and just gave her the money she needed. After three lots of visiting the Bureau de Change, one in Newport Beach and two in Atlanta, in each terminal, she was left with some American dollars, but decided they would have to wait until she got to England.

She put the remainder of the dollars in her carry-on bag in the overhead locker while slipping the bulk of it into the wallet she had hanging around her neck underneath her jacket.

Carrie had refused to tell her friend what time her flight left, so Olivia guessed she might have gone anywhere out of the very busy airport. Carrie even refused to tell her which airline she was flying with.

At 12:45, Flo answered the call in the safe deposit department.

"Hi, this is Olivia Richards. I'm a friend of Carrie Swallow. I just wanted to let you know that she won't be coming back in today."

"Why? Where is she?" asked Flo, who was already very worried about Carrie. She had gone out at about 10:30 and hadn't returned. And then there had been the big explosion to do with Carrie's car. As yet, there had been no report from the police. Nobody knew what had happened or whether anyone was inside the car when it blew up. Many businesses

shut for the rest of the day, and the bank was about to join them. Police had cordoned off most of the parking area and were not allowing people to remove or start their cars in case others had been tampered with, which they suspected was what had happened with the red Mustang.

"Her car has been in an explosion and has been destroyed. Was Carrie in it when the accident happened?"

Olivia was silent for a moment. Shocked to hear the news about Carrie's car.

"No. She's safe. That's all I can tell you, I'm sorry."

"Will you let her know about her car?" asked Flo.

"Yes, I will. I must go."

But Flo wanted to go on talking.

"Was it anything to do with that man who came into the bank yesterday?" Flo asked.

"I don't know - I'm not sure", responded Olivia, trying to hedge away from her questions.

"Well, I believe it was. I don't think she was sick; I think she was scared, and I don't think it was the wrong time of the month because I'm sure she had that only a couple of weeks ago from something she'd said."

"Look Flo. I can't answer your questions because I don't know. Carrie just called me and asked me to contact you and tell you that she's gone. Please can you let the manager know that she is all right."

"OK, but it does seem funny, her going off like that without telling anyone here."

"Thanks Flo – bye."

Olivia got off her phone. She was shaking with the knowledge of the near miss Carrie had escaped from. Who had done it? Was it that man, Joel, that Carrie had been talking about? Now she was glad she didn't know where Carrie had gone to. She just hoped that she was safe wherever it was.

While Olivia was sorting out Carrie's house along with the guys from Capistrano Storage, Carrie made her way across the huge Atlanta airport, taking the shuttle train to the next terminal.

She took herself into a dark bar and hid in the corner, sipping a glass of sparkling water. Time seemed to move quite quickly, because before she knew it, she was being called for her American

Airlines flight to England. As she stepped on board the aircraft, ready to find her seat, she heard one of the Flight attendants talking to another.

"Hey, you come from Southern California, don't you?"

"Yeah - south of Newport Beach - why?"

"I just heard something on the news. Sounds like a car exploded, was blown up or something - killed the driver."

"Really? Whereabouts in Southern California?"

"I thought they said Laguna or something", the younger of the two stewardesses replied.

Carrie stopped dead in her tracks, much to the annoyance of the people behind her.

"Excuse me," she said to the two American Airlines girls. What were you saying about an explosion?"

"Well, it seems strange - but a car just blew up when the driver started it up. At least that's what I think happened. I only caught the tail end of it."

Carrie was feeling very shaky, but she had to know.

"Whereabouts did it happen?"

"I only caught the word Laguna, but I'm not sure."

"Could it have been Laguna Hills?"

"Yes, I think that's right.

Carrie continued, "Do you know what time it happened?"

"I understand - about 11:30 am California time. Why? Do you come from there?"

"No, but my office is in that area. I was just wondering if I might have known the person."

"It's quite a big place, isn't it? So, it probably wasn't anyone you knew," the stewardess replied kindly. "Look - you don't look too good. There is room in the business section. I'm going to upgrade you. You'll be more comfortable, and, in that way, I can get you something to drink right away."

Carrie followed her as if in a daydream. The stewardess couldn't know it - but Carrie was absolutely convinced she did know whose car it was - hers! And she also thought she would have known the driver – Chuck.

Oh God! What have I done? Her thoughts screamed at her. I may have gotten that kind man killed by asking him to take care of my car. And what about Olivia? What happened to her? As soon as I get to London, I'll call her to make sure she's OK.

# Chapter 12

Joel Hernandez and Mungo Fisher later decided to go and check out Carrie's house in the hopes she had returned there, as they couldn't work out where else she'd disappeared to. They turned off the freeway at Crown Valley Parkway and headed towards South Laguna. They were surprised to see a removal van loading up and pulled up just beyond it.

Olivia saw a car stop and intuitively felt something was wrong, and said to the two guys working on the packing – "If they ask you anything, just say you don't know anything about it at all. Say that the lady who owns the place called this morning to ask for you to clear it. She left her keys hidden under a pot by the front door. If they ask her name to say you don't know, but you think she worked for an agency. If they ask where she's gone again, say you *don't* know. And - don't tell them I'm in here. Let them think it's just you - Please!"

"OK - and if they do ask where she's gone, we don't know. Nobody's told us anything."

"Fine. Look, I'm going to hide in the bathroom. Let me know when they've gone."

As Les and Dean carried some more of Carrie's furniture out of the front door, Joel got out of the car and approached them.

"I was looking for the lady who owns this place - but it looks as though she's moving out."

"Yep - that's right," replied Dean.

"Is she in there right now?"

"No," responded Les. "Haven't seen her at all. Just left the keys and asked us to put everything into storage for a while."

"Don't you have a forwarding address?"

"Nope - like I said - don't have no idea where she's gone to."

"And anyway, it ain't none of your business," interrupted Dean. "Now get out of our way and let us get on with our work."

Joel did as he was asked. Back at his car he talked to Mungo. They were puzzled. While they really believed she'd been in the car when it exploded, it didn't make sense she'd called the removal people and asked them to pack her things.

"Hey Joel, it's weird. You followed her into the department store and then she disappeared. You didn't see her come out. Do you think she was on to you and found another way to get out of the building? Maybe they have staff entrances, or something and maybe she went out that way?"

"I followed her in, and she went to the lingerie department and into the changing room and disappeared".

Mungo started laughing, "I bet you really stood out in there. What sized panties were you looking for?"

"Shut up, you thick idiot!"

But by now, the car explosion was all over the radio station they were tuned into. Joel and Mungo looked at each other and wondered who the hell it was who'd died in the car; neither believed it was her.

Still, they didn't really care, and Joel said, "Yeah. We'll just report back to the boss and tell him we've taken the broad out."

Mungo had never enquired what the name of the broad was. He had no interest in her, except that he had a job to do.

Joel had no idea of the name of the boss, and so neither put two and two together and it was only later that Mungo discovered that the broad was actually the ex-wife of their boss Bill Swallow.

# Chapter 13

The American Airlines flight touched down at Heathrow at about 8:30 am. Passengers and crew disembarked feeling weary and a bit dishevelled to go through immigration. The crew members had asked Carrie to hold back and allow other passengers to disembark first, and they would escort her through the terminal to collect her luggage. Carrie then told them she only had the one bag in the locker above her head. They were very surprised, but Carrie ad-libbed and told them most of her stuff was already in England.

After clearing customs, Carrie stuffed her British passport into her pocket. She had already pushed the American one into a side pocket of her bag. She found the two nice stewardess's waiting for her to point her in the direction of the taxi rank. She thanked them and watched them walk away in their smart uniforms.

She hadn't slept much on the long flight across the Atlantic. Fear, guilt, and sadness had all raced through her mind and made it hard for her to make any decisions about what to do when she reached England. She hadn't booked a hotel anywhere, but hoped the cabbie would be able to recommend somewhere. I'll stay in London tonight and get a train down to Devon tomorrow, where my godmother lives.

She was looking forward to seeing her godmother and felt that she would be safe staying with her. However, as Carrie had been unable to contact her prior to her quick exit from America, she had no idea that at the same time Carrie was flying out of Newport Beach, her godmother was just leaving Southampton on a cruise to Australia and New Zealand and visiting many ports on the way.

Carrie thought about calling Olivia, and then remembered she'd left her cell phone in her safe deposit box in California. She also remembered it would be about 2:00 am in the morning, California time, and she decided to postpone her call until later when she reached the hotel.

She stared out of the side window of the taxi as they moved forward. She really didn't feel like chatting, and the cab driver allowed her to sit back in her seat. Traffic got busier and busier, and the journey became slower, almost stop, start. At one point, while the taxi was halted in a stream of cars and buses, Carrie noticed a car parked at the side of a drive with a large 'for sale' sign - £2,000. It was a moment or two, while Carrie stared at it, before it dawned on her that this might be the answer. Leaning forward, she knocked on the window between the passenger seat and the driver. She called out urgently - Stop!

"Please, could you pull over? I want to buy that car."

The taxi driver pulled off the road, turned around, and said, "Sorry, miss, did you say you wanted to buy that car?"

"Yes. I need a car, and I could buy that one."

"Are you sure you don't want to go to a nice hotel and get some sleep? Then you could go to a proper dealer and buy one."

"No! I don't want to go to a garage. Please just wait for a moment while I just check and see if someone is at home."

"Right, miss. It's up to you. Off you go - I'll just wait right here."

"Thank you. I do appreciate it."

He shook his head and muttered, "Americans!"

Carrie let herself out of the passenger door and walked back the 50 yards to where the car was parked. She stepped up to the front door to ring the bell and waited for a few moments before the door was opened by a woman, who could have been somewhere in her late 40s or early 50s. She was accompanied by a barking dog.

"Yes? Can I help you?"

"I want to buy your car."

"I'm sorry, my husband has gone to work. Can you come back this evening?"

"No. I'm sorry, I can't! I need to buy it right now!"

The woman backed up a little. "I'd rather you spoke to my husband. You see, the car belongs to our daughter. She's going on a gap year to Australia and needs the money from the sale of the car. She's away at the moment and has asked us to sort it out."

"I will pay in cash - now. Please, I really do want it," she said desperately.

"Look, can you wait while I phone my husband?"

"Yes," nodded Carrie. "I'll just tell the cab driver what's happening."

Carrie walked forward to the taxi to talk to the driver.

"Are you sure you're doing the right thing, miss?" The older man asked, talking to her as if she were his daughter. "I've got a friend who could find you a nice little car - one that would be safe and in good running condition."

"No. Thank you for your advice, I don't really want to go to London. I'm heading down to the West Country to visit someone, and I could buy this car and drive there today."

"Right you are. If you like, I'll just back up and give the car the once-over for you."

"Please, could you do that! It's very kind of you," replied Carrie. Her mind was turning over quickly now. If she could purchase this vehicle, she could avoid disclosing very much about herself. She knew she was being a bit silly, surely no one would try and kill her here in England - but still, she was anxious to put even more ground between Joel Hernandez and herself.

By the time the taxi had manoeuvred back, the owner of the car was standing at the door waiting for Carrie to return.

"My husband says it's OK. I just need to give you the vehicle licence form, which my daughter has already signed, and then you have to send it off to Swansea to transfer it into your name."

"Fine. Thank you."

"If you've got the keys, I'll just start it up for the lady," the cab driver commented.

"OK. They're here," The woman said, passing them over. She turned to Carrie and invited her to come into the house for a moment to deal with the paperwork.

Carrie followed her into the sitting room and watched the woman who told her that her name was Townsend.

"It's a good car," said Mrs Townsend. "The only reason it's being sold, as I told you, is because our daughter is going away for a year and possibly longer. Her dad has always made sure that her car has been properly serviced and looked after, so we know it runs well."

Carrie counted out the money and handed it over to Mrs Townsend, accepting the papers held out to her.

"Thank you, I'm most grateful," she said as she went out through the front door towards the car and the cab driver.

"It's fine. Looks like it's been well looked after, miss. You should be OK. Do you want me to load your bag into it now?"

"Yes, please," responded Carrie, turning to say goodbye to a slightly stunned Mrs. Townsend.

"There›s a roundabout not too far up ahead", the taxi driver told her. "If I were you, I'd go as far as that before trying to turn round. Then look out for the signs for the M4 - that'll take you down towards Devon. I tell you what, you follow me, and I will take you to where the M4 starts."

"Oh, thank you."

"Also, I've checked the petrol and there's about half a tank, it will take you some way, but you'll probably have to fill up on the way. Don't forget, miss, you need to get it covered for insurance. I use Direct Line. Just give them your credit card number and they will sort it for you."

But Carrie knew she couldn›t do that because she didn›t have any credit cards with her. She had left them all behind in her safe deposit box in California. She thanked him again. Paid what was due and added an extra £50 for his help. She got into the car, feeling a bit strange. She felt as though she should be getting into the opposite side, where the steering wheel was normally placed.

Hesitantly, she moved the car out towards the main road to follow the black cab and join the stream of traffic heading into the city, watched by Mrs Townsend from the front window of her house.

About half an hour later, the cabbie gave her a signal to head towards the M4 while he peeled off at the junction and headed back towards the airport. By this time Carrie felt more comfortable about driving 'on the wrong side of the road'.

It was only later, when Mr Townsend returned home and asked what the name of the woman was, that she realised the buyer had never told her.

"Well, never mind - we've got the money and it's up to her to get the car put into her name," he said as he went off to phone his insurance company, feeling a little uncomfortable about the situation. The whole thing was odd - a woman with a slight American accent, whom he got the impression had just arrived in England, stopped a taxi and bought his daughter's car, and paid cash. Oh well, his daughter would be really pleased!

# Chapter 14

Carrie had time to think about her mad decisions when she joined the M4 to travel west to Salcombe and her godmother›s home. She thought about the impulse a buy a car so quickly and not spending some time in London to get her head sorted out.

Was she mad? Perhaps, but she had so many fears of what could happen to her, she'd acted upon instinct to get as far away and as quickly as possible. She was a bit concerned about not having insurance, but thought that she could sort it out when she got to her godmother's house. Everything had happened so quickly, and she'd had to make decisions very fast, and just believe she was heading away from her problems.

She also made the decision to get a bank account as quickly as possible and credit cards.

The M4 was fairly quiet, and so she travelled at a reasonable speed, without exceeding the speed limit in any way.

She pulled off the motorway somewhere near Swindon to fill up with petrol, grab something to eat, and hopefully find a shop in the motorway services area where she could buy a new cell phone. She needed one to contact her godmother and call Olivia and let her know that she was safe. She was successful in all these things. She tried her godmother›s telephone number again and was a bit worried when there was no answer. What was she going to do if her godmother was out or away? She had no idea and felt that she just had to wait and see what happened. She didn't try to call Olivia because of the time difference. She threw the cell phone onto the passenger seat to use later.

The man in the shop had shown her how to use the sat NAV directional finder. He even helped her to enter her godmother›s postcode so that she could find her way to her cottage.

Leaving the M4, she turned south onto the M5. Another 120 miles to go, but Carrie felt safer every mile she took and was happy to keep on going.

At Exeter, the motorway became the A38 towards Plymouth. Only another 35 miles to go. It had been such a long day!

After what had seemed like a very long drive, she was happy the new cell phone was indicating she should turn off at the next junction, the A381, and signs said Kingsbridge and Salcombe. She was nearly there!

Carrie was amazed at the narrowness of the roads in Devon, and she drove slowly and carefully. At one point, steep banks fell away, and she had trees and woodland on either side. And that›s when it happened. She never did remember exactly how she›d come to crash the car. She slid off the road down the grassy bank, and within fifteen feet, the passenger side of the front of her car hit a tree.

She was fortunate that another driver had seen the accident and quickly stopped. He'd slipped down the bank to where her car was and was glad that it was it the passenger side so severely damaged. He managed to wrench open the driver's door and pull Carrie out. He half-dragged and half-carried her away from the car and halfway up the bank again. It was only then that he called the emergency services for help. As he did so, he heard a bang and, upon looking back, saw the car go up in flames.

It was so hot, and twigs and undergrowth began to catch fire. Henry Banks, the driver of the other car, picked up the young woman, aware that one of her arms hung in an unnatural way, but he didn't have time to worry about it. They both needed to move much further away. Blood was now seeping down from a nasty gash on the woman's head.

The bank was steep, and he needed to put her over his shoulder to carry her up the slope while he caught at branches and saplings to pull them both away from the now smouldering blaze. There was nothing he could do to help her, and he just had to ignore the bushes and undergrowth as he pulled them both to safety. Once he was up on the road, he lay her down on the thick grassy verge and covered her with a couple of blankets from his car. It didn't matter that they were a little dirty because they were normally used for his dogs; she just needed to be warm.

Relieved that she was safe, he sat beside her and thought about what might have happened to both of them. There had been no time to collect any of her possessions from the car, and it looked as though she had lost everything.

It wasn›t long before he heard the sirens on the top road where police, ambulances, and a fire engine assembled. They quickly went to Carrie to see how badly she was hurt. It looked as though she might have broken her arm, and the blood seeping from her head was increasing. The paramedics quickly put a pad over the cut to control the bleeding, and a stretcher was laid down on the grass beside her. However, when they tried to talk to her, she was completely unresponsive.

The paramedics gently lifted the stretcher into the back of the waiting ambulance and prepared to head toward Plymouth, where the main hospital was located.

One of the firemen asked a policeman, who was supervising the accident scene, "What happened?"

"At the moment, we have very little information. All we know is that a young woman crashed off the road, and thanks to the driver of a car following her, he managed to get down the bank and rescue her".

"It must have been a close thing, judging by what's left of the vehicle".

The firemen turned their hoses onto the car and the surrounding undergrowth, but it was too late to do anything. The heat was so strong that not even the paintwork had survived. When the fire was out, all that was left was a black and metal twisted object. It was obvious everything else had gone.

Henry Banks was also in a complete state of shock. The policeman kindly said, "The nearest police station is in Kingsbridge, as you probably know. Are you able to follow us there?

However, it was obvious that he was unable to drive anywhere. They helped him into the back of the police car, and rather than wait for a tow truck to pick up his car and follow them, one of the policemen volunteered to drive it himself.

Another car arrived and pulled over. Deputy Chief Inspector Adam Scott was on his way towards Plymouth to visit his mother in the hospital when he saw the accident. As he got out of his car, an ambulance arrived to collect the injured woman. The paramedics told him they would be taking her to the main hospital in Plymouth, which coincided with where the inspector was headed to visit his mother recovering from a minor operation. He had a quick word with the officers attending, who told him briefly about the accident, whereupon he made a note to contact them later to hear the full story.

At the police station, they gave Henry a cup of tea before beginning the questioning. Henry couldn't give them much information, except to say that he'd seen the car leave the road and slide down the steep bank.

"I managed to scramble down and pull her out of the car and drag her up the bank. Thank God it was the passenger side that took the most damage, otherwise she wouldn't have stood a chance".

Henry shuddered just thinking about what would have happened if he hadn't been there.

"How did you manage to be at the crash site when you did?"

"I've been in Exeter at a meeting all day and was heading home," replied Henry.

"Where do you live? And we will need your name and address, sir."

"Just outside Kingsbridge. I have been following her car for some time. Ever since she left the motorway and turned towards Salcombe. I wasn't in a hurry because I'm tired. I didn't try to overtake her, thank God, if I had, she would be dead by now."

"Please tell us exactly what happened." So, Henry explained everything, wincing as he recalled the details.

"I was just following behind when I suddenly saw the car disappear. I slammed on my brakes, almost sliding off the road myself. I can't remember how I got down to her. I know I crashed through trees and undergrowth. Anyway, I got to the car, had a quick look and wrenched open the driver's door as quickly as I could and just pulled her out".

"After you managed to open the door, how did you get her out? Were you able to undo the seat belt?"

"No. I can't remember. I don't think she had it on, otherwise it would have been much harder to get her clear."

"Why do you think she wasn't wearing a seat belt?"

"I have no idea."

"Do you remember the number of the car?"

"No - but wait, I have a dash cam in my car, maybe that picked up her number, I was behind her for quite a long time."

One of the policemen had already thought this and walked over to the car to check it, and was thankful the keys were still in the ignition because he had to turn on the engine to look at the dashcam, where, sure enough, he found pictures of the number plate. While he was there, he carefully checked the body work just to make sure there were no dents or scratches that might have indicated this man's car had been involved in the accident. He didn't find anything and could only assume the man calling himself Henry Banks was telling the truth

"Did you go back to try and get anything else from the car?" asked the policeman interviewing Mr. Banks.

"No. It was far too hot, and I was afraid the engine would blow up at any moment. All I wanted to do was to get us both away as quickly as possible. In a way, I was glad she was unconscious because I knew it would have hurt the way I manhandled her up to the road".

The questioning went on for a while. Henry gave them all his details, address, and both home, mobile telephone numbers and business numbers.

"I'm afraid, for the young woman's sake, everything she had has gone," said the lead policeman. "Will you be alright getting home now?"

"I think so. It's not far and I'll just take it very carefully."

He asked that they tell him about the girl he'd rescued, and they promised they would.

"We've got all the details, sir, so we'll let you know as soon as we can."

The inspector, having visited his mother, stayed on to wait for the ambulance to arrive and to find out what had happened. While there, he enquired about the girl rescued from the blazing car and was told that they were taking her into X-ray to check for any other damage she might have sustained, but so far, she remained unconscious. He asked whether they had any clue who she was, but the answer was negative.

At the hospital, they carefully removed the clothes the woman was wearing and slid her into a hospital gown before taking her into X-ray.

One of the hospital staff accompanying the patient brought the few bits they had found on the woman over to the inspector. He was very surprised to find that all she had on her was a British passport and about £18,000 in a small bag around her shoulder, and strangely, an odd key hanging on a chain around her neck. Nothing else. He was told her passport had been found in her jacket pocket.

£18,000 was a lot of money to be carrying around and so the Inspector Adam Scott was curious as to why she had so much on her; why she had her passport in her pocket as most people would surely have put it away in a handbag or case; and why was the key so important she had it hanging round her neck? But at the moment, there was nothing they could do because Carrie was deeply unconscious and unable to tell them anything.

With the recovered number plate of the burnt-out car, a detective was sent round to talk to a Mrs Townsend, whose daughter was the former owner of the car.

"Good afternoon, are you Miss Alison Townsend?"

"No, that's my daughter. She's away abroad at the moment".

"Perhaps you can help us. Do you know anything about a car in her name?"

"Oh dear, what's the problem?"

"It's been in an accident".

"What happened?"

"I know very little at the moment. As far as I understand, the car was in your daughter's name. How come another woman was driving it?"

"She stopped outside and told me she wanted to buy the car. You see, we had it on the driveway with a 'For Sale' sign on it. I didn't know who she was, an American accent, I think".

"I need to ask some questions, Mrs Townsend – it is Townsend, isn't it?"

"Yes, I'm Mrs Townsend, but it's my daughter who owns, or rather owned, the car. Oh no, that poor young woman, she seemed to be in such a state when she drove off. Is she alright? You'd better come in, detective. I'll need to call my husband. He'll be better able to talk to you".

"She's alive but unconscious at the moment. That's fine about calling your husband Mrs Townsend, you do that, then perhaps we can go ahead with what happened".

Mrs Townsend put down the phone and said, "he's on his way, but with traffic as it is, it may take half an hour or so. Would you like a cup of tea or coffee?"

"Thank you, tea, milk and no sugar".

They seated themselves at the dining room table, "Right, Mrs Townsend, when you are ready, I'll take some notes".

That seemed to bother her even more.

"I don't know where to start".

"When was the first time you met the young woman?"

"I was in my kitchen starting to peel the potatoes for my husband's supper, and I heard a ring on the doorbell. I went to answer the door, and a young woman was standing there. She asked me if I owned the car in the driveway with the 'For Sale' sign on it. I told her no, it belonged to my daughter, but she was away and had asked her father and me to sell it for her if we could. Then she insisted she wanted to buy it".

"Please, I really do want to buy it, I'll pay in cash – I've got the money with me", had said Carrie.

So, I said to her, "Well, I'll have to talk to my husband, he's handling it for my daughter who is moving overseas for a couple of years. The woman, as I said, had an American accent and said she was travelling into London in a taxi when she saw our daughter's car sitting on the drive. I called my husband to ask him if it was OK to sell it, as the young woman was paying in cash. He said if it was cash and the full amount, as far as he was concerned, it was fine. He told me where the logbook was and said that our daughter had already signed the form, it just needed the date filled in".

The policeman continued to write down what she was saying.

"The taxi driver had parked his taxi a little further along the road and walked back to offer some help. I showed him the garage service documents. The car only had its MOT three weeks before, so we knew it was in good repair, but the taxi driver wanted to look under the bonnet, switch the engine on, and check the tyres. He had a really careful look at the car before assuring the American woman that it seemed to be in a good state of repair".

"And then what happened?"

"Well, I took the money and handed over the DVLA paperwork, which my daughter had already signed. I heard the woman say she was heading for the M4 motorway, which surprised me for a bit, as she'd told me at the beginning she was heading into central London. Anyway, she and the cabbie had a bit of a chat while he showed her where everything was in the car. He then told her he would drive her to his taxi and pull in close behind so that she could follow right behind him. I think he said he would take her to the next roundabout and turn back to lead her as far as the motorway. The last thing I heard him say was to 'keep as close to him as possible and not let anyone cut in front of her.'"

The policeman merely said, "That does seem a bit odd. She didn't happen to mention why she decided to head back towards the airport?"

"No, I didn't hear any more because I went back into my house and shut the door, although I did hear the cabbie telling her she needed to get the car insured. He said she would only need a credit card, and he suggested Direct Line."

"Thank you very much indeed, Mrs Townsend. We'll no doubt be in touch again.

When her husband returned, he asked her what the name of the American woman was, and she said she didn't know because she hadn't been told. It was all very weird, and they didn't know what to make of it.

Her husband asked, "You said something about an accident, Elsie. What happened?"

"I only know what the policeman said, and that was that the car had been in a crash and had been burnt out. I was horrified and asked about the young woman. The policeman said she was pulled out of the car and appears to be unconscious or in a coma. He said he couldn't tell me anything more as he didn't know himself. It's awful, Sam! She seemed like a very nice young lady. I was worried about her, though, as she seemed to be afraid of something. When we were outside, she kept looking around as if afraid someone was following her. The policeman asked me to describe the cabbie. I told him I thought he'd probably come from the airport and was heading into

London. I couldn't really say much about him because there didn't seem to be any distinguishing features except that he was a typical old-fashioned London cabbie driving a traditional black cab – none of these new ones. The policeman thanked me and said they would be in touch if they needed any further information".

Word went out, but it wasn't until much later the next day that they eventually discovered the identity of the taxi driver. He said he was sorry he hadn't been around to talk to them before, but it was his day off and he'd driven his wife to Brighton for the day.

"I know – what you call a busman's holiday! But I don't mind driving, and the missus had a fancy for a bit of sea air. Anyway, what's it all about?"

He'd been very shocked by what the policeman told him about the accident. He'd just sat there shaking his head and saying, "She was such a nice young lady. Very quiet and didn't talk while sitting in the back of his cab, but had been very pleasant when he'd said goodbye to her.

He couldn't give them much more information than they've got from Mrs Townsend. He thought she must have come in on an international flight, but was just very quiet sitting in the back of the cab until she suddenly asked him to pull over to look at the vehicle with a 'For Sale' sign on it. She'd bought it with cash, he told them.

"I was a bit surprised when she pulled so much money out of a little wallet she had hanging round her neck. I tried to look away because it was none of my business. Anyway, I gave the car a good once-over to make sure everything, as far as I could see, was working OK. I reminded her she would need to get it insured, and I pulled out my information for Direct Line and suggested she give them a call as soon as possible. I told her she could do it on a credit card. She said she would when she got to the first service station".

"I understand she'd been heading into the city, so were you surprised when she suddenly said she was heading for the M4?"

"Yes, I was. But she told me she was actually going to Devon to stay with her godmother, and rather than go into London, she thought she would prefer to head west instead. So, I led her towards the M4, and when I saw she was heading onto the motorway, I turned off to go back to the airport. Was she badly injured?"

"Not as far as I know, she was pulled out of the car by another motorist and is currently in the hospital".

"I am really sorry to hear about the accident, I hope she gets better quickly.

# Chapter 15

The inspector thought it would be quite easy to find out about her identity. But it proved to be far more difficult than he expected. Intrigued by a young woman who bought a car from the side of the road and was found only to have a British passport, a strange key round her neck, and £18,000 in a small bag over her shoulder and neck. However, it shouldn't be difficult to locate her relatives.

One of the strange things that came up very early on was that the passport had been issued by the consulate in Los Angeles, and there were no visas or entry stamps in it at all, indicating that it hadn't been used until this trip. Using her date of birth, they tried to track down her family and where she'd lived while in England. There were three or four other women with the same name, Caroline Jane Merchant, but none of them matched the photograph of the woman or her date of birth.

They tried contacting the Consulate for more information but came up against a problem. The Passport had been issued nearly ten years earlier, and the offices then used by the passport people had moved into a new building, and the paperwork couldn't be found.

Inspector Adam Scott was now really intrigued and puzzled. He had been planning to go on a two-week tour of Ireland, but decided to cancel it and stay in Devon and try to sort out exactly what had happened.

He asked himself many questions. Why had she been there? Where was she heading? All he knew from the taxi driver was that she was heading west. But why had she turned off the A38 at that point? This road led towards the coast and places like Salcombe and Kingsbridge, and other coastal villages, but unfortunately, everything else belonging to her perished in the car when it was destroyed by fire. Was she travelling in that direction to visit someone, and if so, who?

They couldn't find anyone in that area with the name of Merchant, and so the inspector could only guess that it must have been a friend rather than a family member. And why so much money? And why was the key? was that a clue? Until she regained consciousness, most of these questions would remain unanswered. Because there were so many questions and strange things about the whole case, the inspector asked for a policewoman to sit beside the unknown woman lying in the hospital bed. It was in the hopes that when she woke up, she would be able to tell them everything that had happened.

It was the amount of money that puzzled him, and where it had come from, and what was she doing with it? The information gleaned from the cabbie and the mother who sold her the car in London had both described her as having an American accent, and the cabbie told them he'd picked her up from the international terminal. So why only English money? Why no foreign currency? Had that been destroyed in the accident? The inspector was beginning to find it frustrating.

In the meantime, they got on with trying to find out where Carrie was going and why. Unfortunately for them, the only person who would have been able to answer those questions was on a cruise ship that left the day before, bound for Australia and New Zealand. She was therefore out of touch with the news taking place in her home county of Devon. She was, in fact, Carrie's godmother. At this stage, everyone was calling Carrie Caroline because that was the name on the passport. It was only weeks later when she blurted out, she wanted to be called Carrie, that anyone knew the name she called herself by.

Over the days and what turned into weeks, the policewomen who'd been sitting with her were unable to report very much. Occasionally, Carrie would call out an anguished 'no'. But as they had no way of knowing what this meant, they simply kept a record.

Deputy Chief Inspector Adam Scott visited almost daily. At first, it was to visit his mother, and after that, he made no excuses for visiting the frail and beautiful young woman, and he knew the feelings he had for her were becoming much more than a desire to know more about her. He knew that he was about 16 years older than her, but he felt he really wanted to protect her. In his heart, he guessed something awful had happened, but as yet, he was unable to find a trace of where she came from and why she was in England; he couldn't be of much help.

Then one morning, a breakthrough came. Carrie opened her eyes and was terrified by what she saw. She couldn't remember who she was or why she might be there. There were all sorts of tubes hooked up to her. As she struggled to move, a nurse standing beside her gently put a hand on her shoulder to calm her down. Word went out that she appeared to be coming out of her coma. Suddenly, the room seemed to fill up with strangers. A man who turned out to be a doctor quietly asked most of them to leave, including the policewoman. He gently began to examine her, but the strange man bending over her seemed to make her even more frightened.

He quietly asked her name, but she just looked at him in terror. The doctor called Inspector James Adam Scott, who dropped everything to rush over to the hospital. But by this time, she seemed to have slipped back into unconsciousness.

Over the next few days, Carrie responded a little more, but it was as if she was afraid to open her eyes and see what's around her. Gradually, she stayed awake longer. The inspector tried to gently question her, but this seemed to make her more upset.

"Caroline, can you remember who you are"?

She had no memory of anything up to the moment when she opened her eyes, and as if to blank it all out, she closed her eyes again and went back into a deep sleep which nobody could draw her out of.

Days went by, and she began to become more aware of the people around her. She did everything they asked but remained virtually silent.

Every day, they hoped that her memory would return, but she showed no sign of it happening. The Inspector tried showing her passport with her name in it, but all he got was a blank stare. The young woman seemed to have no idea who she was.

When questioned about where she was going and who she was going to see, again, nothing. It was only when the inspector brought the key on the chain into the hospital that she reacted, and a flicker of fear appeared to cross her face. Something had made her frightened, but nobody could work out what it was.

The inspector had sent photographs of the key to all sorts of departments, but the only thing anyone could agree upon was that it looked like a key for a safe deposit box, but of course, nobody had any idea where to find that box.

Day by day, she began to understand the routine in the hospital, but for the moment, this was her life. The young American woman had nothing else to hold onto. Nursing staff helped to get her washed, breakfast, and then usually, Carrie went back to sleep. A physiotherapist came every day and began to put her through a series of simple exercises to build up the strength in her body. Councillors and therapists were brought in, but the problem was that with most people, their memories could be gently jogged with photos and stories from their pre-coma state, but with Carrie, they had nothing. Specialists from other hospitals and the private sector were asked for their advice but were unable to help – all anybody could do was to sit and wait and hope that nature would perform a miracle.

A speech therapist had also been called in to help her, and that, and listening to the staff words, came rapidly back, but still no memories of anything since she'd woken up.

One of the nurses suggested that perhaps they should get her some normal clothes to wear because she couldn't go on wearing hospital gowns or the nightgown someone had given her. The inspector asked one of the young policewomen, who was about the same age as Carrie, to go and buy some clothes that would be suitable for a woman of her age. He gave her about £300 and said if this wasn't enough to please ask for more.

Bags of new clothes from a number of shops were placed on Carrie's hospital bed. They included tracksuits, new trainers, and T-shirts, which were much more sensible when working out with the physiotherapist. Also, a couple of fun jackets and sweaters, plus underwear, nightwear, a lovely fluffy dressing gown, and make-up. Carrie was delighted with the outfits the policewoman had chosen, but still felt very uncomfortable not knowing anything about her past. The next time the inspector called in at the hospital to see Carrie, he almost didn't recognise her when he found her sitting up in a chair beside her bed wearing some of her lovely new things. The policewoman had gone over budget, but Adam didn't mind at all.

She was getting daily physiotherapy treatment and doing well because she was a good patient and did everything that she'd been told, but however much the staff tried to help her to remember things it was just a blank.

Inspector Adam Scott never mentioned the money found on her because he wasn't sure of the effect it might have. At the moment, the money was safely locked up in a box at the police station. He also discovered the car hadn't been insured in her name, and he guessed that she hadn't had time before the accident. Of course, he didn't know at that point that she would have been unable to insure the car because she had no credit cards with her. Carrie had left these behind in California because they were all in her married name, albeit no longer married to the man whose surname she had, Bill Swallow. Adam only found out about these things after her memory returned.

More worryingly for him, he hadn't managed to find any family or friends to come forward to help her when she was discharged from the hospital.

And although her godmother had returned from her cruise, all the publicity had long since died down, and she had no idea that Carrie was still in a hospital in Plymouth.

Before she left the hospital, Carrie suddenly asked Adam to call her Carrie. She just blurted it out one day, and when Adam asked her why, she told him her name was Carrie. She said nothing else to explain why she wasn't to be called Caroline.

Adam talked to his mother, Anne, about Carrie and asked what he should do.

"Mum, I don't know what to do. She should be leaving the hospital very soon, but where is she to go? Carrie still has no memory of anything that has happened, or even who she is. I don't think putting her into a care home would do her any good, and she couldn't go into a flat or cottage on her own, it wouldn't be safe".

Anne replied, "What if I moved in here, into your cottage, and we bring her home. You have plenty of room for all three of us, and I could look after her while you are at work. You know your hours are erratic, and so bringing in carers wouldn't be feasible".

"I had been thinking of bringing her here, and my mind has gone round and round as to how to manage it. She's too frail and with no memory and so she wouldn't be able to cope anywhere else. Do you mean it, Mum? It would certainly be weeks, if not months."

"Yes, I do mean it. How long do you think they'll keep her in the hospital?"

"Another couple of weeks, but no longer than that. They've more tests to do on her head, but apart from that, she is improving daily".

"Right, we have time. First, let's go and have a look at the bedroom we'll put her in. It is probably like the rest of your house, a bit masculine. We will need to make it ready for her".

"Thanks, mum".

As they walked around the house, his mother, Anne, made sensible suggestions.

"Do you know of any painters or decorators who could come at very short notice?"

"Yes, old Bob Lewis has semi-retired, and I am sure he would do me a favour. I helped him out when some fly-tippers dumped a load of stuff on his field, so I'm sure he would help me out at short notice. What had you got in mind?"

"Something pretty and feminine. Could you get him over here so that I can talk to him before I go home?"

Adam called the old man who agreed to come immediately. While they were waiting, Anne began measuring the windows for new curtains. When the old man arrived, Adam's mother started to explain what she wanted.

"Get rid of the dreary wallpaper first and just paint the woodwork white. Everything will go with that. Can you work out how many rolls of wallpaper we will need, Bob? In the meantime, Adam, I will drive into Plymouth first thing tomorrow morning and take myself to Debenhams to look for curtains, sheets, towels, duvet covers and so on. I'll take the measurements for the windows and hopefully, be able to find some ready-made ones that will fit. If not, I'll get some fabric and run them up myself. As you know, Adam, I have made many curtains in my time. I will also look for some pretty wallpaper".

"Mum, you're a star. You have no idea what a weight you've taken off my shoulders".

On several occasions over the next two weeks, Adam brought Anne to visit Carrie. The two of them seemed to get on well together. It was Anne who told Carrie about their plans for her.

"Carrie - Adam and I have been talking about where you could go after they release you from the hospital".

A look of fear crossed Carrie's face.

Anne lent across and took one of Carrie's hands, "It's alright, we have decided to take you home with us. Not to my house because it isn't big enough, but Adam's has plenty of room. I am planning on moving in to take care of you, especially when he is working. You will have your own room and bathroom, and I'll be in the bedroom next to you".

Carrie gave them both a little smile and said, "Thank you".

As Carrie continued to improve in the hospital, things were moving ahead in Adam's cottage. Over the next few days, Adam's mother helped him to prepare the room for Carrie's arrival.

"What do you think?" asked Anne as she showed her son the new things she'd bought.

"Very nice, mum. I'm not much into feminine things, but I love the colours. I'm sure Carrie will too".

New bedding and matching curtains replaced the rather masculine things Adam had in his spare room. She added some bright cushions and a new rug for the floor. It looked lovely and fresh and ready for its new occupant.

"What do you think of the bathroom?" Matching towels and bathmats completed the colour scheme.

"Love it. Thanks, mum, for all your hard work".

Anne also bought some lovely, scented bath gel and shampoos and arranged them around the bath and filled the house with flowers. When everything was prepared, they were ready to bring Carrie home, along with the very few things she had, mostly those bought for her by the kindly policewoman.

It had been two weeks of hard work before Adam and his mother were able to go and fetch Carrie. As they pulled up at the front entrance, they were greeted by many of the staff who were waiting to say goodbye.

Adam's mother went into the hospital to fetch Carrie, while Adam stayed at the front door chatting to some of the staff. Carrie was in a wheelchair being pushed by one of the young male nurses, although she had protested, saying she could manage without a chair. Anne walked beside the chair as she accompanied Carrie to the front door of the hospital, where Adam was waiting for them next to his car. A number of staff, those who were able, were also there to say goodbye to the girl they only knew as Carrie. So many of them had become very fond of this beautiful young woman, and they hoped very much that she would soon regain her memory. Lots of them were even in tears when they said goodbye to her.

Anne sat in the back beside Carrie, who just couldn't take her eyes off the scenery they were passing. As he drove, Adam thought about the whole situation. He was worried that leaving the hospital might make things more dangerous for her, in fact, for the three of them. He had no idea what to watch out for. He kept thinking, who or what is she frightened of, that she was frightened wasn't a doubt in his mind. Something had happened, and it was as if the memory loss was a natural effect of blanking out whatever bad had taken place.

Later, Adam sent a thank-you card to everyone in the hospital who had helped look after Carrie, along with a hamper of chocolates and cakes. It wasn't much, but he didn't know what else to do.

Anne had arranged for a personal trainer to come to the house a couple of times a week to help Carrie improve on her walking as quickly as possible. Both she and her son knew they were in for the long haul.

Over the weeks, little bits of information began to come out. On one occasion, when Carrie and Adam visited a garden centre to buy compost for some tubs for his patio, they headed towards the coffee shop, where Adam was planning to buy them lunch, and as they went past the glasshouse area of the garden centre filled with exotic shrubs and plants for sale. Carrie suddenly stopped and went over to where a dozen gardenias were potted up. She cupped her hands around one of the flowers, leant over and began breathing the scent in deeply.

"Oh look! Don't they smell beautiful?", but when Adam asked if she remembered them from somewhere, she just shook her head.

Next, she reached out for a lemon tree standing within the citrus fruit area. Adam noticed tears running down her cheeks, but had no idea about what she was thinking. In his mind, he guessed the scent was triggering off some forgotten memories. Picking up the largest gardenia, he put it in the trolley, planning to buy the fragrant shrub in the hopes that it might be a breakthrough to what was hidden in her brain.

Another day, when his mother Anne was preparing dinner for the three of them, she noticed Carrie in the garden with a pair of secateurs. She was cutting off the dead heads of the roses and pruning one or two other plants. Anne was intrigued by this because this hadn't been something she'd been taught to do since her accident, and so it must be a throwback to things she had done in the past.

"Gosh, Carrie, you really have an eye for gardening, especially for pruning and dead heading the roses. Your green fingers must have come from somewhere". Carrie just frowned as if to say she didn't know where.

One day, when Adam was driving them towards Exeter, a bright red sports car overtook them. He suddenly realised that Carrie had crouched down in the passenger seat and was almost whimpering with fear. Again, he had no answer.

He pulled over and took her in his arms, "It's alright, I'm here for you, I won't let anyone hurt you again".

He still knew so little about this beautiful girl and longed to be able to take her fears away. The problem was that he had no idea who or what had hurt her. He had almost no more clues now than he'd had at the beginning. A passport, the money and the key were the only things. That and the sudden request to call her Carrie. Again, the questions he kept asking himself were, who is she and where does she come from. He knew it was the States, but it was such a vast country that it could have been from anywhere.

Adam had to go to Manchester for a police conference and took Carrie with him. While there, he decided to take her for dinner in the very colourful Chinese section of the city. He hoped that she loved Chinese food as much as he did. Their table was in the window, and so they were able to look out and watch a very colourful procession go by, headed by a huge Chinese dragon. He pointed this out to Carrie and told her that it could be for a wedding or some other celebration. For some reason, the word dragon made her draw back in her seat. For no reason at all, Carrie began to write down the letters RT in her notebook. Adam asked her why the initials RT were important, but Carrie could only shake her head, saying she didn't know.

Nothing made sense. Adam made notes of everything that had happened in the hopes that the answers would come soon. He felt that it was like putting together an extremely difficult jigsaw puzzle without any edges.

Adam was very frustrated that he couldn't find out who she actually was. He had tried all sorts of things. One of the first things he did was to see if she had any relatives in the United States, but as he had no clue where to begin, she could have come in on a number of International Airlines from the states, or elsewhere for that matter, and he wasn't even sure if she came from there. He tried to search under the name of Merchant because she had to have some family somewhere but as he didn't know the first names of her parents, he came to a halt very quickly, And he couldn't know that her mother had deserted them about 12 years before and gone back to Australia where she came from, had remarried and so had a different name.

"Carrie, when we were in the Chinese restaurant, you wrote down the letters RT. Can you think of any reason why those two letters are important?"

"No, I can't. Oh, Adam, it is so hard. I keep trying to remember things, but nothing comes through".

# Chapter 16

Carrie's specialist at the Plymouth hospital suggested that Adam take her to the National Hospital for Neurology & Neurosurgery in London to have some tests done. They needed to find out if there were any reasons for her loss of memory. She would have to stay in the hospital for a couple of nights, and as the dates coincided with a police conference on illegal immigrants, Adam took her himself.

He booked first-class tickets on the Plymouth to London train before hailing a taxi and heading for the hospital, where they had to go through the form-filling and admittance, before meeting Mr Doug Wallace, the consultant. They were shown into Mr Wallace's consulting room by an efficient-looking nurse.

"Good morning, I'm Doug Wallace, and you must be Carrie", he said, shaking her hand, "and Inspector Scott?"

"Adam Scott, we are hoping you will be able to solve Carrie's memory problem", said Adam, reaching out a hand to the other man.

"Please sit down, and I will explain the procedure and what tests we will be doing. "We will be performing a brain scan. Don't worry,

Carrie, it doesn't hurt, it's just very noisy. Have you ever had an MRI scan?"

Adam nodded, "When she was first taken into the hospital in Plymouth, but I'm not sure she will remember it".

"It's a bit like that, except it is just the head. It will take twenty to thirty minutes and take multiple pictures of your brain to see if there is any damage or reason for your memory loss or why it is still happening".

Eventually, Adam left a very forlorn and frightened-looking Carrie. His heart ached at leaving her sitting on her bed wearing the hospital gown supplied to her.

Adam had his own thoughts, and on his way out, spoke to the consultant, "Could she be unconsciously blocking some sort of terrifying experience?"

"What sort of experience?"

"I don't know. All I am guessing is that something happened prior to the car crash, something that frightened her so much she was trying to escape. The trouble is, I have no way of knowing whether I am right or wrong. I don't even know who she is, and of course, I have no way of jogging her memory because everything, apart from a few small things, was destroyed when the car she was driving crashed and exploded. I have tried showing her the British passport we found in her pocket, and she just looked blank. For some reason, the key, we now believe, belongs to a safe deposit box, seemed to disturb her and she had a large sum of £ sterling in a small bag around her shoulder – nothing else".

"Thank you, inspector, I'll bear what you've told me in mind. I'm going to get my team assembled now and see what we can find".

Adam returned later on that evening to find a rather drowsy Carrie. According to the sister in charge, she had become very agitated, and so the consultant had prescribed something to calm her down a little.

"How are you feeling?" he asked Carrie.

"Not good. Oh, Adam, I am so scared. What if they find something really wrong with me and I never get my memory back?"

"I'm convinced you will be OK. Another day here and then I'll fetch you on Friday to travel home again. Hang in there, my brave girl. We need to get you fit and well again".

Upon his return to collect Carrie on Friday morning, he was waylaid by the sister and was asked if he could wait a few minutes before going in to collect Carrie.

"Mr Wallace wants a word with you. I'll let him know you are here, and he'll come up straight away".

"Good morning, Adam. I wanted a word with you. First of all, we found nothing that could cause the memory loss, no damage, and so I am coming round to your conclusion. Something happened during our testing. A couple of our nurses were chatting quietly, and one was telling the other about a planned holiday. She mentioned that she and her family were flying to Southern California and were visiting Disneyland. Carrie went rigid at the mention of Southern California. Then she put her hands over her eyes as if to block out something and, in what I would say was an anguished voice, began to say, 'Arty, I'm so sorry it was my fault. Oh Arty! When we asked her what it meant, all she would say was – I don't know! I can't remember! And the conversation ended there".

"Arty? Could it have been the initials RT?"

"It could have been, I just thought it was someone called Arty, short for Arthur, maybe you're right".

Adam went on to explain Carrie's strange behaviour in the Chinese restaurant. They had to end the conversation because Adam was conscious of the need to get to Paddington station for their train. He thanked Doug Wallace and said he would keep him up to date with Carrie's progress.

Inspector Adam Scott made a mental note to get Interpol involved with trying to find out about anyone living in Southern California whose names began with RT.

# Chapter 17

They made the trip to Paddington train station with plenty of time to spare. Adam carried both their bags, just small overnight ones, and after helping Carrie into her seat in the first-class section, was just reaching up to place their bags into the overhead space when Carrie let out what sounded like the noise a child would make mixed with a muted scream.

"Carrie, my love, what's wrong?"

"It was him, no them, walking past the carriage – out there on the platform".

"Who?"

"I don't know. There were the two of them together. One of them saw me and pointed me out to the other. I can't remember their names, but I saw them! The first one who saw me recognised me, I'm sure. He stopped for a moment and just stared. He then grabbed the other man's arm and pointed at me".

Adam had paused with loading the luggage up onto the overhead shelf and, for a quick moment, saw the two men. One was fairly tall and dressed in jeans and a jacket, with an expression of shock on his face. The other, rather stocky, had darker skin, maybe South

American, his face almost contorted with anger and disbelief, and his body language looked anything but pleasant.

"Were they people you knew from your other life?"

"I don't know – I don't know!"

Carrie was sobbing by now, and other passengers looked concerned.

"It's alright", Adam told them, "She's had some bad news".

Several passengers murmured something consoling.

"Carrie, can you tell me anything else?"

"What if they're on the train and are looking for me?"

"They won't find you. Look, Carrie, I want you to go through that door and into the lavatory. Take the bags and don't open the door until I knock four times. Four times – you understand. Anything else, stay locked in. We are going to leave this train".

With that, he almost pushed her through the open door. "Now, lock it".

Carrie could do nothing but go along with Adam's demand. She was very relieved when the knock came because it had seemed like hours.

Adam jumped off the train and, seeing a guard standing there with his flag ready to wave the train away, Adam stepped in front of him and showed him his police identification, while explaining he needed to get his wife off the train – not bothering to explain she wasn't his wife.

"My wife saw someone staring at her through the carriage window. Someone she is terrified of and is afraid might be looking for her right now. She was bothered by a stalker a few months ago and is afraid it might have been him. She has locked herself in the lavatory and won't come out until I fetch her. First of all, I want you to hold the train for a few minutes. Then, please, can you collect some of the staff, porters, if you like. I want to try and hide my wife in a group of people so that we can walk her out onto the main concourse. I am assuming you have a police room somewhere in the station?"

"Yes, sir. You stay there. I'll contact the driver and fetch some of the lads. How many do you think?"

"At least half a dozen and with you and me - that should be plenty. You won't have to delay the train long. And can you contact the police room and get someone to come over to the platform entrance to meet us?".

"Yes, sir", replied the guard.

"As soon as you assemble the staff, I'll get back on the train and bring my wife out, and if you could gather on the far side of the door away from the exit gate that would be perfect, we'll step down and you can then hide her amongst you".

The guard got very busy. Firstly, he held up his red flag to show the stop sign to the engine driver, and then began collecting several of his colleagues. As soon as they were in place, Adam climbed back on board and tapped hard four times on the lavatory door.

Adam grabbed the bags in one hand while reaching out for Carrie.

"We have a group of staff waiting. I want you to step down onto the platform and let them form a protective circle around you. I'll be there with you as well. We are going to leave the train and will, for the moment, be escorted into the police room in the station".

Carrie looked as though she would have fallen, she was so stressed. Adam glanced behind and found that the door into the compartment had automatically closed, and as far as he could see, there was no one behind them, so he stepped off first and leant back to take her hand and help her down among the group waiting.

As he stepped back on to the platform he glanced towards the front end of the train in time to see two men further along the platform who seemed to be arguing, with one of them pointing to the other train along the other side of the platform, and if he could have lipped read he would have seen the younger, taller man say – 'That was my ex-wife, Carrie. Wonder what the hell she's doing in England?'

The two men split up, the taller one heading for a sign in the distance saying 'Underground' while at the same time the darker, shorter one climbed onto the train Adam and Carrie had just left. Adam said a quick, Thank God they'd managed to get off the train before it started to leave.

Adam would have smiled had he known that the man who joined the train had caused a number of passengers to complain to the ticket collector. The man had gone backwards and forwards through the train several times while staring at everyone. The collector searched for him and, eventually, upon discovering he didn't have a ticket, heavily fined him before escorting him off the train at the first stop. It was only later, when Carrie remembered who the two men were, that the significance of the sighting was to spur on events not planned at the time.

Almost immediately, the train began to pull away, leaving Adam and Carrie, and their protectors. One of the ticket collectors said, "It's alright, Miss, we won't let anyone get near you. You just stay tucked in amongst us".

The small group led her out through the exit gate, but Carrie couldn't help turning round to see if 'he' was following her. However, it was impossible to look through the group of kind men wanting to make sure she was safe.

Through the gate, they were met by one of the station police personnel who conducted them down a discreet passage and into the police room where Carrie was handed a mug of hot tea while Adam told them briefly about the encounter. He had already decided to hire a car and drive them back to Devon as he was afraid Carrie might not cope with a train journey. While they were waiting for the car to be delivered, Adam chatted about football – anything to stop Carrie dwelling on her experience. He had time to discuss what had happened when they got home.

The journey home took much longer than the train, but at least Carrie felt safe. Adam had called his mother to tell her what had happened, and while she was very concerned, she said she would see them when they arrived – and she'd have a bottle of red wine opened and ready.

The next morning, after Adam had gone to his place of work, Anne sat down with Carrie.

"Adam hasn't said much, but how did the hospital visit go?"

"They couldn't find anything major wrong but said it was more likely to be trauma. Not quite sure what that means".

They chatted on for a bit before Anne asked, "Would you like to talk about what happened on the train?"

"I feel such a fool. I'd just sat down in my seat while Adam put the bags up above. I was looking out of the train window when I caught sight of a man staring at me. He'd stopped and was just standing there looking, and he had another man with him. I know he recognised me, but I don't know who he was. I can't remember, I just think both he and the other one are really bad, or nasty. Anyway, I panicked and let out a cry. Adam immediately became concerned and told me we were getting off the train".

"Do you think he or they were someone from the life you can't remember?"

"I don't know. Oh, Anne, it's awful! I think I must have known the taller one, but I *can't* remember. My mind is a complete blank, but somewhere in the back of my mind, I think the other one was a bad or evil guy, and the moment I saw him, I was terrified".

"Tell me what you can remember about them".

"It was only for a second that I looked at them. The taller one somehow seemed out of place amongst the British train travellers. That quick glance made me think he was perhaps American?"

"What made you think he was American?"

"I don't know. His clothes, I guess. It was the other one. I'm sure I met him somewhere. I felt he would kill me if he could. You see, I didn't know if they were planning to get on our train or the one on the other side of the platform. Adam made me lock myself in the lavatory while he sorted out a 'posse' to get me out of the station. I was so scared, Anne, and I don't know why. I stood as near to the door as I could so that I would hear Adam knock – and then I thought – what if he gets off the train and it begins to move, and

Adam doesn't have time to get back on? What would I do? What if *they* were on the train and watching to see which station we get off at? I began to panic again. I was so frightened. At this moment, I don't who or why anyone would want to hurt me, I just feel someone is after me. It might be easier if I knew who, but I don't know or if I ever will".

All Anne could do was to hold her in a big, warm hug and reassure her she was safe with them.

Anne didn't ask anything much more, but she was very concerned for Carrie's sake, especially after Carrie had confided in her that she was afraid the man might have searched for her on the train and even found out where she was now. Anne quietly closed the curtains and made sure all windows and doors were locked. She was very thankful that Adam had installed a sophisticated alarm system with remote controls that went through to the alarm company, which could alert the authorities if needed.

She was mentally making notes to pass on to Adam when he returned home later. He was very much delayed. A yacht laden with packets of cocaine and other drugs had sailed into Falmouth harbour, where customs officers had been waiting to seize them. The haul was huge and so involved some extensive police work, arresting not only the boat's crew, but also involving other agencies, including the Metropolitan police who'd heard about the shipment and were also waiting for the boat to dock.

Anne was still up when Adam got back, and they sat and talked quietly about the train experience. He also told his mother what the consultant had said about Carrie overhearing a conversation between two nurses and how she'd reacted to the mention of Southern California.

"I think it might be a small breakthrough, Mum. Apparently, Carrie seemed startled, as though she was in shock. The consultant also said she had been almost whispering to herself and repeating Arty and 'it was my fault, I'm sorry'. I couldn't help remembering, when we were in the Chinese restaurant, her writing the letters R and T in the notebook she always carries around to jot down any thoughts she might have that would give her clues about her past, and I am wondering if the two match up – southern California and those initials".

"What are you going to do?"

"First thing tomorrow, I will get on to some colleagues in the Met and see if they can put out some feelers. The trouble is that I don't have the proper name or even know if RT stands for a man or a woman. But I do think it might be a tiny step forward".

As it happened, it was harder than Adam thought, and it took several days to get a response to his query. Two things came up. One was that a woman named Rose Tremaine, known as RT, had been brutally murdered in her apartment, and it appeared the murderers had been searching for something other than valuables, although her jewellery was missing, but the police seemed to think that was an opportunist move.

The other curious thing he learnt was that almost a year later, a young woman named Carrie Swallow had just disappeared. Her best friend had no idea where she'd gone and nor did her workmates. Her friend seemed to believe Carrie was safe somewhere, although she did say it was odd Carrie hadn't been in touch with her to let her know how she was, as she'd promised to do. Also, the young woman's car, a red Mustang, had been blown up in the car park outside the bank Carrie had worked at. A mechanic who came to drive it back to his garage had sadly lost his life in the explosion.

The inspector murmured to himself, 'That explains why she was so frightened when that red sports car overtook them on the motorway'.

The thing that puzzled Adam was her name. Her passport said Merchant, and yet her friend called her Carrie Swallow. Odd!

Adam didn't know what to do. Should he tell Carrie what he'd found out, and if he did, what would be her reaction? She might be curious, or she could be upset thinking he had been checking up on her. He decided the best thing to do was nothing until he'd had a word with her consultant, Doug Wallace.

This took longer than he hoped. Both of them were busy men, and as the question wasn't urgent, Adam left it until they had some free time to chat. When he finally got through, he found the medical professional a bit hesitant.

"To be honest, inspector, I've never come across a case like this before. Are you in any hurry to expose the truth because if not, could you delay it in the hopes her memory comes back, which could happen at any time – or never?".

"No, I don't have to talk to her right now. I think I'll take your advice and wait. Thank you for your help".

"How is she, by the way?"

"I didn't tell you that after we left your hospital Carrie had a nasty shock on the train home", and Adam went on to tell him about the strange men on the platform and how Carrie thought she might have known them in the life she knew before her accident.

"She's OK but certainly is more nervous than she was before this happened".

"It's a strange case. Normally, we have a background story of a patient's life before the memory loss to work with, but you have nothing. Anyway, to reiterate, we found nothing wrong with her brain. I personally think it is just time, but if you find she is becoming more anxious about her past, perhaps you could introduce her to small hints at a time and not throw everything you know at her at once. Give her time to become used to little bits".

# Chapter 18

L ife went on in the small family unit of Adam and Carrie, and his mother. Adam was exceptionally busy with his work, while Carrie and Anne pottered around shopping and gardening, which she was pleased to see Carrie enjoyed a great deal. Anne also taught her to cook some of Adam's favourite British meals which made him happy.

However, Anne confided in Adam that she was concerned about Carrie. She went out with Anne but had stopped going to the village shop on her own and had even given up cycling after mentioning her fear that someone knew where she was and was watching her.

As things were progressing, Anne began to spend a bit more time having lunch or coffee with her friends, but only on the days Adam was able to be with Carrie.

Adam began taking her out to different places that he loved. One beautiful day, he drove them to a small village in Cornwall overlooking the sea.

"Before my father died, we came most summers to this little village and stayed in a cottage. We swam in the sea, played in the rock pools, hunted for crabs amongst the seaweed, and my father revelled in doing barbecues for us. Then I'm afraid he got cancer and by the time they found it, it was too late. He was only seventy-two at the time. By then, I'd joined the police force and was based in London".

They bought Cornish pasties from the same shop Adam and his parents had for years and took them onto a low hill overlooking the water, where they sat on a bench watching the people enjoy the sandy beaches below. Adam pointed out the rock pools at one end of the beach. As they watched what was going on, a light aircraft, a few hundred feet out from the coast, flew past them. It was quite low, and they could clearly see the pilot in the cockpit.

Carrie suddenly drew her breath in, almost choking on her pastie, while she watched the little plane. Suddenly, for no reason at all, it was as if the floodgates partially opened. Haltingly to begin with, as if tiny memories were thrusting themselves forward in her mind, and it began to slip out.

"Adam, I think I know who that man was, the one on the platform".

Adam remained quiet while she searched for words.

"I am pretty sure his name is Bill Swallow".

Adam almost recoiled at this. She was related to him. But of course, she didn't know he already knew her name was really Carrie Swallow. This had been confirmed during his investigations and was something he hadn't told her yet.

Adam was relieved at the former.

"It's not surprising he recognised me, although I haven't seen him for some years. He was bad! I should have listened to my father, who tried to persuade me not to marry him. He was my former husband".

Carrie became much more agitated and incoherent as she stumbled from one thought to another. Things began to come out in a jumbled way, mostly about her early life and her parents.

"My father met my mother in London, where he was a student, and she worked for an English family as an au pair. She came from Sydney, Australia. They married when they were young. My father was twenty-three and my mother was twenty-six. I was born a couple of years later, in London".

Carrie paused here as if to try and recapture further memories.

"I can't remember why they decided to move to America. Probably because I was too little. Anyway, things went downhill after the move. My mother was always a bit wild, and I think, embarked on a number of affairs. Then one day, she just announced she was going back to Australia. She'd already packed in her job and left permanently three weeks later. I remember my father was really upset. I should really let him know I'm alright".

If Adam was right, her father was already dead.

She began to close up again as if blocking further memories.

"Carrie, can you tell me just what happened a little while ago? Was it the airplane flying past? Did that jog you and bring back some memories?"

Carrie just nodded and said, "My dad taught me to fly".

Adam was about to ask more questions when she interrupted, "Please, Adam, can we just leave it there for the moment. My mind is sort of screwed up. It's as though the mist or fog is sliding over my brain again. I have to allow myself to go over things in my own mind".

"Of course. You take as long as you like. I'm here for you. I don't mind if it's little snippets over the next days or weeks".

It was several days later. Adam had managed to get away earlier than usual, and his mother was at a neighbour's playing bridge. He and Carrie finished supper and were sitting together finishing a glass of red wine, when Carrie said, "I think I'd like to tell you some more".

Adam waited for her to speak. He already knew a lot more about her life, but was still suppressing it to give her time to open up. It wasn't that he didn't trust her, he did completely, it was just that now that he knew a lot more than she realised.

"You know, I said I had to let my father know I'm alright?"

Adam nodded.

"I remembered – he's dead. He was driving home from a holiday in the mountains when a crazy driver forced him off the road and down a wooded slope. They said he'd died instantly. The driver of the other car also crashed – drink driving – anyway, he got twelve years in jail for manslaughter. But it didn't bring my dad back".

Carrie continued, "After mom left, dad and I did everything together. He took me to my tennis lessons, and then when I started to play soccer, he was always there on the touch line shouting instructions with the rest of the dads. Quite often, we'd go with some of the other parents and their kids to a pizza place after the game. It was fun!"

She paused for a moment, a frown across her face, "I loved him so much, Adam, and although he was my dad, he was also my best friend. Sometimes we'd go to concerts together, and often to the movies. We used to go up into the mountains over the holidays to ski, and a couple of times we went to big baseball games together in L.A. I missed him, and still do, so much".

# Chapter 19

Adam had asked the American police for further information about the murder of RT. He'd been sent reports of what had happened. He now knew that it had been Carrie who'd found the old lady, and he privately thought it must have been one hell of a shock for her, but it couldn't have been that which caused the trauma because the killing had taken place nearly a year before Carrie travelled to England.

He knew that Carrie had been taken in for questioning because, at the beginning, the police thought she might be involved or even have carried out the brutal murder. Throughout the interview, a tough female California cop pushed her hard, but she told the same story each time, and upon following up her alibis with friends, it was shown that she wouldn't have been anywhere near the old lady's apartment at the time of the killing. In the notes, it said that her friend Olivia, one of the witnesses, had come the following day to collect her and had taken her back to her own home.

Adam planned to contact Olivia himself to find out more. He'd got her contact details from the local police in California.

Carrie had gone quiet again, and Adam thought it was unlikely he would get anything else that evening. He wanted to ask her more about her past, but was still following the consultant's advice to leave things alone at the moment.

A few days later, Adam decided to do as the consultant had suggested, to give her tiny hints about RT to see if they jogged any memories.

"Carrie, do you remember writing the letters RT in your notebook? Can you think why those letters are important?

"No. I am sure they are, but I think they are linked with something really bad that happened."

Adam left it there, hoping his words might stir something else.

A few days later, while they were watching a report on television about the visit of the Vice-President to 10 Downing Street, the UK Prime Minister's residence, Carrie suddenly sat bolt upright and pointed at the screen,

"Who's that?"

"It's the Vice President and our foreign secretary.".

"No, I mean the man standing near the Vice President".

"I don't know. Do you?"

"Yes, I think he's the other man on the platform - and he's a murderer. He killed RT. I'm sure it's him", she said with her voice getting quieter with every word.

Adam realised this might be another breakthrough. She had suddenly mentioned RT for the first time. He put the TV on hold to look closer at the man. He certainly reminded him of the swarthy, shorter man he'd caught a brief glimpse of at the railway station

"Can you remember his name?"

"No. I can see it all clearly. He came into the bank to get something out of his safe deposit box, and when he dropped it, it came open, and I saw - the bracelet. It was her's. She called it something to do with a dragon. He threatened to kill me next! Adam, I'm so scared".

As if she remembered, "He grabbed my arm and twisted it, and then threw me on the floor. I was so frightened, I think I just lay there in the corner until he'd gone. I know it's him - on the TV. I'll never forget his face, and he was on the railway platform with Bill. I don't understand. Why were they together? Adam, do you think they have traced me to England? Are they looking for me?"

"Carrie. I don't know why they were there, or if he is with your Vice President, but I'm certainly going to ask a lot of questions. Please sit there, I must make some phone calls. I'll be right back, but if you need me, just shout and I will come".

Adam knew it was a bit pointless to try to find out more about the mysterious man; all he had to go on was Carrie's statement that he was a murderer. She was still going in and out of her memory loss and had no idea who he was, and the belief he had killed someone in America, but no proof. Neither the US nor the British police would do anything. However, Adam thought it was worth trying to find out who he was and what he was doing in Britain, so he put a call through to a friend in the metropolitan police who said he would do his best to get an answer.

As Adam walked back into his sitting room to rejoin Carrie, he thought back to the meal in Manchester at the Chinese restaurant.

She had seemed startled by the huge dragon in the parade outside and had begun jotting down the letters RT. Things were beginning to make a little sense.

"Carrie. You mentioned RT. Can you tell me anything more about her?"

Carrie remained silent for a few moments.

"She was kind, and what you call people like her in England, eccentric. I'm trying to remember where I knew her. I think it must have been where I lived or worked – I think it must have been southern California, because I haven't lived anywhere else since I was little. I keep getting tiny pictures, and then they are gone again. Will I ever get my memory back?"

"Yes. I'm sure you will. Every day, you are remembering a little more. Don't feel pressured. Doug, your consultant said memory is odd, sometimes the loss disappears suddenly, and with other people it can take time, just as yours is".

A few days later, Carrie asked, "Adam, was I in a car accident?"

"Yes, do you remember anything about it?"

"Where did it happen, and where was I going?"

"You were heading towards Kingsbridge and Salcombe. As to where you were going, I don't know, but I suspect you know someone in that area".

"I think I do know. My godmother lives there and I think I may have been going to see her. Do you know why the crash happened?"

"No, you just went off the road. One curious thing, Carrie, the man who rescued you says you were not wearing a seat belt; don't you normally wear one?"

"Yes, of course, I always fasten my seat belt. I just had a memory of the crash. I am sure I bought a new mobile phone somewhere. The man showed me how to work it and to set the directions on it so that I could find my godmother's house. I can't get it out of my head that it started ringing. I really panicked because nobody could have known the number. I seem to remember the phone was on the seat beside me, and I tried to reach over to see who it was. The phone had slipped to the far side, and I couldn't reach it, and I have a faint memory of unclipping the belt. So, I think I must have undone it, and that is all I remember. Everything is black after that".

"That makes sense to me. I understand now how the accident happened".

"Adam, whose car was it?"

"Yours. You bought it from a family on the way into London. That we do know. We know you flew into London and were in a taxi on your way into the city when you saw a parked car for sale, and according to the cabbie, you insisted he stop his vehicle, and you bought it. He said he checked it over and it seemed OK, so I don't think it was a problem with the car, but reaching across to grab the phone could have caused you to lose control, especially as you were driving an unfamiliar car on the left-hand side of the road. Something most people in the world find strange".

"Have you found my godmother?"

"No, because we don't know her name. It is odd, though, because after the accident, it was all over the news and press, but nobody came forward. Can you remember her name?"

"Yes", said Carrie as she gave it to him. "I'd like to go and visit her".

"Please wait for a little longer. I don't want anyone else to know where you are. You told me a little bit about RT. Do you know her real name?"

"It was Rose Tremaine. She told me she was laughed at in school, the other girls called her Rose Tree, so she called herself RT".

Carrie interrupted herself, "So much is coming back. I remember she came into the bank where I worked, and we got talking".

Adam made a note to ask her more about the bank, but was happy to allow her to chat on about RT.

"I'm not sure now, looking back, but I think she must have moved into the area fairly soon before we met – or maybe she chose us as a new bank, which is strange, because it was about twenty-five minutes at least from where she lived. It's odd because I am only now wondering why she came to us. It could have been that we had a huge safe deposit section. I never thought to ask her".

A week or so later, Adam decided it was time to show Carrie the key that had been found hanging on a chain around her neck.

"After you were rescued from the car crash, all we found was this key, a British passport, and the money. Can you remember anything about them? Everything else you might have had was destroyed in the fire along with the car. Nothing was left".

Carrie took the key and held it in her hand for a few moments, her face screwed up into a questioning mode as though she was trying to conjure up pictures in her mind.

"It reminds me of the keys we used in the safe deposit department in the bank".

"Why do you think you kept it, and why is it important?"

"I guess it might be the key to my box. I'm not sure because they were all identical. Why is it important? I can't remember. Maybe I left something there?".

The following evening, when the two of them were out for dinner, Carrie suddenly said,

"It's coming back. It *is* my key. I seem to remember going round to RT's apartment after we'd been out for dinner. She'd taken me to a lovely French restaurant in the town. She loved French food, she said. During dinner, she regaled me with stories of some of her wilder behaviour".

A smile lit up Carrie's face.

"One of the ones she told me made me laugh. She was invited to a party at the British Embassy in Paris. It was a very grand affair and one of the Royals was there – a Prince, I think she said. Anyway, he was rather good-looking. Tall and dark hair with a charming smile – and no, she didn't tell me his name. She said she decided to seduce him, after all, she'd slept with an American President, and so a royal Prince was nothing out of the ordinary.

I had to laugh at this. She asked the man who'd taken her to the embassy party to introduce her. She wasn't in a relationship with him, he preferred men to woman, and RT rather thought he fancied the prince himself".

Carrie paused here to sip her glass of wine before continuing her story as told by RT.

"I was taken over to meet him, and I could see he was interested immediately. Even as a young girl, I was very good at getting any man

I wanted. I am not sure what it would be called, maybe sex appeal? Some people have it, and most don't. I had it in abundance. I'd already used it many times in my life and knew exactly how to turn on the charm. I only had to look into a man's eyes, and they were gone".

Adam was fascinated by these disclosures and asked Carrie to continue.

"RT told me the prince had nodded away other people waiting to speak to him and that he and RT moved into a smaller side room to talk. RT said she put on all the charm she had. She said that after all, having run a very successful escort agency, she knew all the tricks of the trade and certainly turned them on him. After a little while, the prince spoke briefly to his equerry, or whoever he was, and we were discreetly ushered out of the building by a side door where a car was waiting for us".

"Carrie, I'm shocked! Did she know who she was seducing?"

"Oh yes. She knew exactly who he was, and as he was married, she preferred it to remain confidential."

"So, what happened next?"

Carrie lowered her voice a bit so that Adam had to lean across to hear what she was saying.

"It gets a bit saucy here, so I'm not going to talk so loudly. Don't want other people at other tables around us listening in. RT told me she took him back to the palatial apartment she was renting. She laughed when she said her bedroom was like a 'tart's boudoir'. She thought it was owned by some Middle Eastern billionaire, and this was the suite he brought women to. The walls and ceiling were covered in gold, and the draperies were silk. Going on, RT said, apparently the prince really thought he was something special, but I soon showed him he really didn't know very much at all".

She added, "I'd been a working woman as well as teaching younger women how to really turn men on, and in some cases women as well, although she said, I personally was not interested in that side of sex. To be fair, he was pretty good, and I enjoyed the night as much as he did. I taught him some wild things and he said at one point he didn't know what was happening, his head and his body were literally 'exploding' with sheer pleasure".

"I wish I'd met her", Adam broke in.

"Yes, I wish you and my dad had met her. Oh, both would have been fascinated. I wish my dad were still alive, I know he would approve of you".

Adam smiled while Carrie continued, "She told me lots of other things, but I'm not sure I can talk about them. It was almost dawn when he left, RT said. I told him to let himself out. I have no idea how he got back to the hotel where he and his entourage were staying".

Carrie giggled at this, "She seduced a prince of the realm and then turfed him out on the street! I almost think she was forgetting who I was and was instructing me as she had done with other 'girls' under her wing".

"The story doesn't end there. A couple of years later, RT was taken to a Garden Party at Buckingham Palace, and she told me that during the afternoon, members of the royal family came out to walk in a parade among the guests".

"They do. I've been to a couple of garden parties there myself".

"Well, she was one of the guests drawn out of the lines of people. I don't know if this is true, but she said a number of the guests are invited into the passage made down the middle of the lawn, and as the royals walk down, they are introduced".

"Yes, that's true. So, she was one of them?"

"She was, and the first person she met was 'the royal prince – from Paris".

"What happened?"

"RT told me she'd dipped a slight curtsy and then looked straight into his eyes. His mouth curved into a slight smile, and then he said in a voice only she could hear – 'thank you'.

"What a story! Carrie, you are an extraordinary woman. What happened next?"

"She went on to tell me more about her wildlife and how she used to go on trips, skiing and travelling the world with various lovers. The senator was the main one, but he was married, and in any case, they, she and he, had a very open relationship, and he didn't mind if she was with someone else. The only rule was that, when he was available, she dropped whoever she was with and joined him. She said it worked remarkably well".

"It wouldn't suit me".

"Me neither. Anyway, it was that evening she took me back to her apartment and opened up about the much more serious things in her life, which she said she thought were coming to an end. I asked her if she was sick, with cancer maybe, she said no, she just felt they would be coming for her soon. I asked who she meant, and she just replied – 'the bad guys."

Carrie had become much quieter and more serious.

"I didn't really believe her, thought she was having 'old age' thoughts, but when she said she knew so much about so many people whose lives she could damage, I began to listen. RT started to open drawers, one of which was a concealed drawer in a big old-fashioned cabinet. She showed me it could only be reached when a side panel was pulled out to release the mechanism. In there, she had lots of papers and some photographs. She asked me to take them away and put them in a box at the bank. Proof, she said, of bad things done by some of the influential people she'd come across over the years. Routing among her extensive bookcase, she pulled out folders that looked like traditional books, but were in reality, journals, diaries, and notebooks. These she also handed over to me to put somewhere safe. From elsewhere in her bedroom, she brought out many more pictures and photos. I was fascinated, but also a little cautious because many of them were of famous men and women, and in a few cases, what looked like underage girls with much older men. I was rather shocked by these".

"So, what did you do?"

"I took them with me and the next day I rented out, in my name, one of our largest boxes and arranged them in it. RT seemed very relieved when I told her".

She said, "Don't tell anyone you have them because it would be dangerous for you. Especially, never tell the police because I don't know how many of them are implicated".

"After another evening out dining, when RT had had more to drink than she should have done, she talked about Hollywood stars, more than one of whom died under questionable circumstances, and including mafia bosses, who were linked with at least one of her lovers. I seemed as though she knew or had met everyone, from the middlemen drug dealers right up to the President".

"No wonder she was concerned. It sounds as though she had a right to be frightened".

"She did, and it cost her her life".

Adam saw the sadness in Carrie's face, and his heart went out to her.

"Adam. There's something else I've remembered. That same evening, when RT gave me her papers, she also gave me a key and a code. She had, what she called, a vault, in Philadelphia. She'd lived there for many years before moving to California. What she had already given me was only part of the things she's hidden away. Nobody knows this except me, and now you".

"You didn't tell the police or the investigators?"

"No. That was one of the things RT stressed, not to tell anyone like that as it would probably be dangerous for me".

"Where is the key and the code?"

"In my box at the bank".

"So, you have no idea what's in the vault".

"No. Even more explosive than the stuff she asked me to look after, I guess. Possibly recordings and tapes. It could be information and truth about assassinations or heavy money laundering, or even blackmail and threats hanging over people. I just don't know. All she would say was that she had knowledge and information that could still hurt people".

"So, the intruders and killers wouldn't have found much when they broke into her home?"

"No. They made a terrible mess tearing things apart, so, except for some jewellery, they would have found very little. RT told me that one of the high bosses in the mafia, who gave her lots of papers and pictures, had said to her that if she was ever short of money, all she needed to do was to go into the box and pull things out at random and use the information for blackmail. Several of the people whose secrets were hidden in there would pay millions not to have the information disclosed. She never had to use this, in her own words, thoughtful advice. She said that the person who gave her the stuff was killed in a hit and run accident, which was deliberate".

"What a waste of a life!" added Adam. "One day, and it may be sooner than we think, we have to go and clear the boxes".

Carrie just nodded.

Adam asked, "What happened to the crooked senator? I'm assuming he is no longer alive".

"No, he was shot down when he was on a trip to Texas. RT said it was almost certainly an assassination. Apparently, he had sensitive knowledge about the then-President. Nobody was charged. The story was that the killer escaped, but RT said it was more likely to be an inside job that was pushed under the carpet".

# Chapter 20

One evening, soon after the revelations about RT and her life, when Adam decided her memory had returned sufficiently, he took Carrie out for a quiet dinner and proposed to her. She accepted immediately.

In the meantime, Carrie took some driving lessons and passed her test. Strangely, she wasn't afraid of driving because she had absolutely no memory of the car crash she'd been involved in, and so wasn't frightened of driving a car. Adam had told her enough about the accident for her to feel comfortable behind the wheel.

A few weeks later, she and Adam were married very quietly, with just his mother there. Now she could change her name to his, and Carrie Merchant or Swallow could disappear forever.

They went about changing everything, a new passport, a driving licence, and they opened bank accounts and got her new credit and debit cards. The money Carrie had brought with her from the States went into the new bank accounts. All in the name of Mrs Caroline Scott.

At his mother's suggestion, Carrie changed more than just her name. She had her hair cut much shorter and highlighted so it was more honey coloured than dark. She was also quite a lot slimmer after the hospital stay than she had been when she arrived in England. Arriving home after Carrie's trip to the hairdresser's, Adam was astonished to see the new Carrie. He put his arms around her and gave her a big hug.

"You are so beautiful, my darling wife, I love you", he told her.

Another evening, when they'd gone to the local pub for dinner, Carrie asked about Adam's past life.

"You know everything about me now, but I don't know a lot about you, Adam. Please tell me about you as a child and growing up, and what happened."

They were sitting at a small round table near a big open fireplace with logs burning on it. Adam lent over and took her hand.

"I have been waiting for you to ask me, and I guess one of the things you want to know is whether I have been married and divorced? The answer is no. I was engaged for some time when I was much younger. I thought she was the love of my life, but now I realise that it's you." He smiled at her as he said this

"You want to know what happened, don't you? Well, I guess a policeman's salary wasn't enough for her. One day she just walked out, and before I knew it, she was going out with somebody much wealthier than I was."

"Did it upset you?", asked Carrie.

"For a while, and then I realised that she hadn't broken my heart, just my pride."

"Where were you living then?"

"In London, when I was in the Metropolitan Police. Over the years, I have seen pictures of her in newspapers and on television.

Blonde and brassy and turning up in expensive holiday resorts, socialising with other people of the same desires and wearing larger diamonds and smaller bikinis. I look back and realise I had a lucky escape."

"How and when did you move to Devon?"

"My current boss is Chief Inspector Steven French. We worked together in London and did some active tours in Northern Ireland. He is a number of years older than I am and at the time had a wife and three children. He decided that London was no place to bring up children, crime was on the increase, and when the job came up down here, he applied for it and got it. I stayed where I was working my way up the ladder in the Met. Then one day, the job opened up in Devon. His previous deputy Chief Inspector was retiring, and he contacted me and asked me if I was interested. I immediately said yes because I'd grown up in Somerset, the next-door county, and my mother lived down here. So, I packed up everything in London and joined my friend Steven, and I have never regretted it."

It appeared that Carrie's memory had just about returned, and over the next few weeks, they talked at length about what they could do and decided that at some point, they had to return to Southern California to open the safe deposit boxes locked up in the bank where she'd worked. She was the only one who could get into the boxes - he now knew that she had two. Both in her name, but one of them containing papers and diaries given to her by the old lady known as RT. He guessed that these held many secrets which could be very damaging to both living and non-living celebrities in many varied occupations, from presidents and prime ministers, mafia leaders, people connected with Hollywood and gangsters tied up with trafficking, drug cartels, private yachts and islands where the rich and fraudulent men and women met up to socialise.

They decided it would be California first, and then the vault in Philadelphia after that.

By this time, his mother, Anne, had returned to her own cottage, staying long enough to make sure that Carrie could manage without her. Adam had bought Carrie a small car, and so she was able to do all the shopping. Before Anne had left, Carrie had asked her to write down some of his favourite recipes.

Adam lay awake at night, wondering what the hell he and Carrie could do about going back to California, knowing that it could be very dangerous and possibly fatal to them both. One of the first things they did was to destroy her old English passport, leaving that part of her life behind her.

Carrie was becoming less fearful, although the odd thing could send her off – such as the new postman who reminded her of her ex-husband. The first time she saw him approaching the letter box, she ran and hid in their bathroom, locking the door behind her, just as she'd done on the train, to protect herself. Another day, when Adam was at home, he introduced themselves to the postman who turned out to have a soft Somerset accent, totally unlike the harsh voice of Bill Swallow.

Adam decided he needed to talk to his boss, Chief Inspector Steven French. They discussed this, and Carrie cautiously agreed he should go ahead. He had to be open with the Chief Inspector, he told her. At first, she was terrified of telling anyone else about what had happened to her, and became quiet and subdued, so Adam left it for a few days until she told him to go ahead.

"It's OK, Carrie, I completely trust the Chief Inspector. I've known him for over 20 years. We were together in Northern Ireland during the troubles. We faced bombings and ambushes when we were dealing with the IRA. I would trust my life to him!"

The next day, Adam made an appointment to meet up with his boss. Upon entering his office, Adam closed the door behind him before the two men greeted each other with the close friendship they had.

"What now?" asked the Chief Inspector.

"It's about my wife, Carrie".

"I didn't know you'd got married. I suspected it would happen sooner or later". His boss held out his hand, "Congratulations, I am absolutely delighted for both of you".

"We kept it secret because Carrie is still a bit paranoid about some people in California. Only my mother was present".

"Go ahead and tell me what I can do for you".

"As you know, she was in a very bad car accident several months ago and was in the hospital for several months while she was still in a coma".

"Yes, I do remember that and that you took a personal interest in the case and her".

"The problem we had was that we didn't know who she was. All she had on her when she was pulled from the wreckage was an English passport, £18,000 in a small bag hung round her neck, and a key on a chain. The key turns out to belong to a Safe deposit box in

Southern California. When the car came off the road and crashed, it caught fire, and everything else connected with her was destroyed in the subsequent inferno. I tried to find out who she was and where she was from, but it was impossible. I couldn't even work out where she was going. We asked for information from anybody who might know her in Great Britain, but nobody came forward, and Carrie can't remember anything between leaving the bank she worked for in Southern California and her memory returning a few months after she left the hospital over here. She remembers nothing."

"OK. So, I ask again, what is the secrecy? You obviously have much more to tell me."

"Yes, Steven. I'll try to start at the beginning and keep it as brief as I can. It goes back to Southern California when Carrie worked in a bank. She befriended an old lady who confided in her and told her all sorts of things that linked the old lady with senior politicians both here and in the United states, the mafia, gun running, money laundering and anything else connected with organised crime" Adam smiled before he continued, "even a royal prince, and no, I don't know which one".

"This sounds as though it's going to be a long discussion. I think I could do with a coffee before we really get into it. How about you?"

"Yes, I would like one."

When the two of them had a cup of coffee in front of them, the inspector looked straight at James and asked, "Do you personally think this is all true, or is it some wild imagination on her behalf?"

"No, I don't believe that Carrie has made all of this up. In fact, I totally believe everything she has said, and it is much more serious than we have ever taken part in. At the moment, I can't prove any of it. I believe that the documents and papers, and diaries she has described that are hidden in the safe deposit box hold a great many dangerous secrets. By dangerous, I mean those people who have been involved in many vile acts. Of course, most of these people, the old lady implicated, are already dead, some from old age and others probably taken out by their mafia bosses. I do know from among the names Carrie has told me, certainly one of our senior people worked in the foreign office and the Home Office, was actively engaged in covering up terrorists, and the money passed hands to shield certain people."

"Carry on, Adam, you've certainly got my interest".

"Carrie has said there are photographs of the old lady when she was much younger. Apparently, she was a mistress of a crooked senator, and she mixed with presidents, Hollywood stars, and high-ranking mafia organisations. But as I've said, many of them are dead now, including Carrie's old lady, who was brutally murdered and Carrie found her. It was obvious that it was no accident, and it wasn't just a burglary; they were definitely looking for something else. They didn't find much because the old lady had put everything into Carrie's keeping. She told Carrie she knew that they would come for her one day."

"Any idea who she meant?"

"I think all the answers will be found in the safe deposit box."

Adam and the Chief Inspector talked on for several hours."

"What do you want me to do, Adam?"

"I want you to give me leave of absence. I'm not sure how long it will be, but Carrie and I are going back to Southern California to open the boxes. We would prefer to fly out from somewhere like Manchester and head to Vancouver. We don't want to fly into an American airport; Carrie is still afraid that someone will find her. We've taken precautions and everything, all her personal documents are now in her married name. Mrs Caroline Scott. Carrie Merchant, as she was when she arrived in this country, is virtually non-existent. The only people who looked at her old passport and might have seen her surname are very unlikely to have remembered it."

"OK, how soon do you need to go?"

"I think in two to three weeks. I have some sorting out to do before we leave."

"You said you prefer to go from Manchester, and I can help you there. I will arrange for a car to drive you to the airport. You would of course fly upper class, and I will put in a request for your fares. We'll just say that you're travelling on police business."

"I've checked it out", said Adam, "we can go by Air Canada. From there, we plan to hire a car and head south towards Southern California. Carrie is afraid of flying into any American airports. I have tried to reassure her but understand her fears."

"Right, get the details to me and I will fix it for you. And good luck. You know that I'm here, Adam, at the end of a phone line. Just call me if at any time you think I can help."

With that, they gave each other a brief hug, and Adam left the building.

Back at the cottage with Carrie, they began to sort their things out for the long flight. They both went together to see his solicitor to make new Wills in favour of each other. They also visited Anne to let her know they were leaving on holiday. They told her they weren't sure how long they were going to be away, but again, they would be in touch.

Carrie reached out for her mother-in-law and gave her a big, long hug.

"Thank you for everything, Anne. I couldn't have got through all of this without you. You have been absolutely wonderful."

Anne was feeling a little tearful and found it hard to say anything in reply.

"Just come back soon, I will be waiting for you both," she said as if sensing this trip was more than a mere holiday. She'd heard enough from both of them to know there was a lot more to Carrie's background then she'd been told.

# Chapter 21

Adam's friend, the Chief Inspector, had been as good as his word. Almost three weeks later, they were picked up very early one morning and driven straight to the airport in Manchester, where they were escorted directly through to the departure gate and met by an Air Canada official who led them into the upper-class section of the aeroplane.

Once seated, Adam took Carrie's hand and held it tightly. The flight was long, but they were able to sleep for some of the way.

Touching down in Vancouver, they were met by more officials who discreetly led them to the Hertz hire car area. Formalities completed, they set off towards the hotel they'd booked into for a couple of nights before beginning the long drive south.

Carrie became quite panicky as they headed towards the Canadian border with America.

"What if someone has tipped them off that we are coming? What if they are waiting on the other side to arrest me!"

"They won't have a record of your new name against your previous one. We are just a British couple who are leisurely driving south through Washington and Oregon on our way to California, so don't worry, my love. I am here to protect you".

"Adam, you don't know how bad they can be. Remember I told you about my car being blown up in the car park? They wanted to get me, but they didn't care who else got hurt – or died. Also, I have never told Olivia I'm OK. I hope nothing bad has happened to her".

Adam decided this was a good time to reassure her. "We have been so busy; I haven't got round to telling you I have spoken to Olivia. Just a few days ago. I got her number from the California State Police. I think I told you I had asked for the documents connected to the murder. I haven't wanted to jar your memory with horrible thoughts, so I have played down what I know. Olvia's name came up on the police documents about the evening of the murder. They went into a lot of information to do with the finding of the body and taking you away for questioning. Do you remember any of that?"

"No, not much. I seem to recall a horrible woman cop, I think she tried to bully me into confessing I had something to do with the killers. All I could say was what had happened".

"Olivia's name was among the papers as an alibi for you, and the person who came and fetched you from the police station. I've known about her for several months, but held back telling you because I knew you would want to call her and, at the moment, we don't know who, or if anyone, is watching her in the hopes you will give yourself away. I wanted to try and remove all traces of the old Carrie and replace it with the new Caroline Scott, which I believe we have".

Carrie remained rather subdued. "Have you spoken to her yourself?"

"Yes. I called her on a phone connected to the police, so that if anyone tries to follow up, they'll get a shock when it is answered. I never mentioned your actual name, just that you're a friend of hers. She understood. I was very careful about what to say, except you'd had a car accident and lost your memory, but are now physically fit and well again. She's happy and just said to give you her love. I did ask her if she was alright, and she told me she'd had some scary times soon after her friend (you) disappeared. She didn't know if it was a coincidence but felt she was being followed on several occasions, and of course, there had been a terrible incident in the car park. I told her I knew about that and briefly asked if the feeling of being watched was still going on. She said no, she didn't think so. After that, I said goodbye. Didn't say a word about our visit, because we don't know if someone is still spying on her".

Nothing untoward happened, and taking their time to travel, they were able to check into small motels for the night, mostly ordering takeaways to eat in their room. Carrie was too paranoid to go into bars and restaurants, even though Adam assured her that she looked nothing like the old Carrie. He also thought she wasn't in a hurry to get to the bank. He had taken to call her Caroline in order to confuse anyone looking for a Carrie.

It took them a couple of days to drive through the states of Washington and Oregon before entering California. They shared the driving and kept strictly to the speed limits as they didn't want to be stopped by the Highway Patrol.

Adam asked Carrie to tell him more about the remarkable story of RT. What came out absolutely astonished him and almost made him wince on a number of occasions, so graphic were her descriptions.

"RT was amazing. I think sometimes she forgot who she was talking to, especially after several dry martinis, straight up. We often went out for dinner, and those were the best times to get her going. She really made me laugh when she told me a story about a man in his fifties – she must have been in her seventies by then. He suddenly asked her, 'What age do women stop wanting sex?'. Her reply, or so she said, was 'I don't know – but I'll tell you when I do!' RT was amused that he was a little shocked".

Carrie continued in RT's comments, "I did offer to help him. Come over to my house and I will teach you what to do to make your wife excited and keen. But he didn't come, and the last I heard, his wife had gone off with someone else. A shame, I could have taught him so much".

She was so open and frank, and she made me laugh so much.

RT continued, "I much prefer younger men, preferably half my age. Those of my age are usually past the kind of sex and love making I enjoy, and yes, in case you wonder – I love sex. Always have done and probably always will, and over the years, I have perfected it. In fact, when I think of some of the older men I've dated, I shudder; they were always anxious that they were giving me a good time, which mostly they were not. Once they have done, they usually want to go to sleep, or when the Viagra wears off, they are as much use as 'a limp fish on a marble counter'.

Carrie burst into laughter when she recounted this.

Suddenly, RT seemed to recollect Carrie's age, "You did say you were married, didn't you?"

Carrie nodded and said, "Married and divorced".

"How was it? Was he good?"

"No, awful!"

"Then I am not surprised you got rid of him".

"She gave me a lot of good advice too. She told me she was sure I would find a good man one day, someone I wanted to spend my life with". Carrie turned and smiled at Adam when she said this.

RT went on, "I never wanted to be with just one man, I loved the variety and the excitement of the first seduction. The different beds and often other places we got together, all added to the excitement. Always thought I would get bored tied to one person, so I never allowed it to happen. naughty. When he opens the door and finds you wearing stiletto heels with just a feather boa draped round you, he's going to forget dinner and sweep you into the bedroom. As we used to say, 'Jazz it up!' Keep him guessing – and let him find interesting ways to turn you on too".

Adam felt his face turning a little red. Carrie continued to open up. Too many couples do get frustrated and look for other partners outside of their relationships. It's the excitement that never wears off on the first occasion. Honey, this is my advice: don't ever let your man get bored with you. Spice up your life. Imagine him coming home after a long day's work, just wanting to eat dinner and then fall asleep in front of the television, when you are dying to have some fun. I suggest you do something wild, and about the stories the old lady had told her.

"She told me about some of the wilder places she'd had sex in. Believe it or not, that included Air Force One, the president's plane – and in his bed, of all places. She said it was with the senator - that was before he was assassinated, but on that occasion, she was accompanying him on a trip across the country. The senator was a little shocked that I knew the sleeping area so well, but I told him Mr President had 'shown' it to me himself."

Adam asked, "Is the President still alive?"

"I am not sure, RT was very discreet about his name, but if he is, he's no longer in office. Shall I go on?"

"Please do. I am fascinated with RT, although not sure she was right in telling you some of her wilder memories".

"One other thing she talked about, and seemed very disturbed by it, was the only time she allowed herself to go on a trip to a private island with some multimillion-dollar older men and a group of very young, most of them still teenager girls. She said she was disgusted. She knew quite a few of the men who were high-profile and well-known on the world scene. Much as she herself loved sex, she hated what these horrible, gross old men were up to. The girls were used and abused by a bunch of narcissistic, depraved creeps. She had flown with them to the island by private jet and so was forced to stay on the island until the rest of the party were due to leave. RT had tried to talk to some of the girls, who admitted they hated what they were expected to do – but most of them had come from abusive homes, mostly poor, and they believed they were meeting with people who could help them get into the movies or whatever and earn millions of dollars. She said she tried to describe what would happen when the men grew tired of them and threw them back out onto the streets. Sadly, for RT, they were living their dreams, as sordid as they were, and wouldn't listen to her. It is so sad, Adam; she was such a vibrant woman and would probably still be entertaining lovers if it wasn't for those savage killers".

# Chapter 22

After skirting around Lake Tahoe where some of her ex-husband, Bill Swallow's relatives lived, they drove along roads with little traffic and through small towns and villages, when Adam noticed a gas station and coffee shop and, as there were no other cars outside, he pulled over and said he was ready for a coffee and maybe some fried chicken the shop was promoting.

Carrie was afraid of going too close to the town of Tahoe, a place where she and her dad had skied several times during the winter and spring, and although probably none of Bill's relatives would have recognised her with her short blonde hair, she couldn't risk it.

She and Adam got out of their car and entered the rather run-down establishment, where they found a good welcome from the owner and his wife. They were amused by the décor, which looked as though it had been there for fifty years, which they agreed, after meeting the owners, it probably had. Shelves with dusty books and old photos of the gold mining days sat alongside battered tin mugs, and cracked dinner plates adorned the walls. When their dinners arrived, they were relieved that they were dished up on clean, modern dishes.

After serving their chicken and creamed potatoes, and a beer for Adam, the old man lent against the bar.

"Where are you folks from?"

Carrie replied, "We just came in from Canada", while Adam said, "We're from England".

At that, the old man became chattier.

"That's really interesting. I thought I recognised your British accent", he said to Adam. I had a guy in here a few days ago, and he was telling me a real interesting story. He said his name was Bill something – "Oh, I remember, Swallow. He was heading to visit his folks from hereabouts."

Carrie froze, and the colour faded from her cheeks.

Adam just said, "Do go on with your story".

"Well, it was like this", he said, "the guy who stopped in here. He told me he'd gone over to England, London, I think it was. Anyway, he was with a friend, and they were catching a train from some big rail station, when he was walking alongside one of the trains that stopped there, he looked up and saw his ex-wife in one of the railcars. Just sitting there. Well, he looks at her, and then she sees him, and he recognises her. He said he pointed her out to the guy with him, who also knew who she was. The other guy said, 'What the hell, she's supposed to be dead.' This guy, Bill says, "That's what you told me! You were paid to take her out, and you obviously lied".

Carrie had stopped eating. She pushed her plate away, and Adam knew he had to get her out of there but needed to know a bit more.

"What happened then? Where did the Bill guy go?"

"The guy says the other one wanted to get on the train and look for her, but when I looked again, she'd gone, and I wondered if I'd really seen her. Anyway, we had a bit of an argument, and I left him to catch another train to head for the airport and that's the last I've seen of him".

"Have you ever seen him before – or since?"

"No sir. He hasn't come this way before. The coffee shop owner looked at Carrie and asked in a kindly way, "You alright, lady? You don't look too good to me".

Adam replied for her, "Just tiredness, I guess. It's a long drive from Vancouver".

Adam got behind the wheel as they prepared to head further south, and as they drove further south on highway 395, Carrie gradually became more vocal.

"Adam, what if Bill goes back into the coffee shop and the owner tells him about us? He's bound to guess".

"I'm sure that won't happen. The old man said he'd never seen him before, and so it is unlikely your ex-husband will go back there".

But they were wrong. The next day, Bill Swallow returned to the diner and the owner told him all about the couple who'd visited the previous day.

As they headed south, Carrie seemed to put the experience out of her mind and began to point out various places she wanted one day to show Adam.

When they passed the sign for Bodie, Carrie told him the story of the old, abandoned gold mining town. He was fascinated. They thought about turning off to visit the abandoned 'ghost' town, but agreed that they could wait for another day. A bit further South, Carrie pointed out the signs for June Lake. This was where they had planned to stay overnight. Adam checked his rearview mirror as he turned the car right off the highway and saw that there was nothing behind.

She had already told him about the first time her father had driven her there, and as they were approaching the town on the lake, she had seen a sign saying 'Oh Ridge'. Wondering why anyone would have called it that, it wasn't until they went over the Ridge and saw the beautiful lake ahead of them, surrounded by mountains and aspen trees growing on the sides of them. She had instinctively said 'Oh! '

"I had planned to buy a cabin here. I was going to come and ski throughout the winter and in the summer walk along beside the streams that link one lake to another and maybe do a little fishing for the rainbow and brown trout living in these waters."

Adam was enchanted by these ideas and hoped one day she would get her wish. He kept her talking about her dreams in the hopes she would put the coffee place behind her, although, knowing her as well as he did, he guessed it was very much on her mind.

They stayed in the main hotel in the little town of June Lake, their bedroom window looked across the lake to the hills behind, and each with a glass of wine, they watched the sun go down, casting huge shadows across the water. Sitting in a corner of the dining room, they were both astonished by the size of the steaks being brought out from the kitchen. Neither of them had believed anyone could eat a 32-oz steak, but it appeared there were some diners who could.

The next day, late in the morning, they rejoined Highway 395 with the huge Sierra Nevada mountains towering up into the sky, up to 14,000ft in places, with Carrie driving this time. Adam knew the first settlers had crossed these mountains to the softer coastal plains and wondered how they'd done it with the old horse-drawn wagons and marvelled at their bravery. There seemed to be very few places where they could get through without going over the tops of the mountains.

If they had known, Bill Swallow was turning off the main road towards June Lake. He'd remembered Carrie and her father's love of the town filled with log cabins. He'd already made the turn when he saw the car with Canadian number plates. The make and colour matched the coffee shop owner's description. He wasn't able to turn around quickly and had to head towards the town before finding a suitable place. Back on the highway, he quickly put his foot down to catch up with them, only to find a huge truck and trailer carrying logs had turned onto the road ahead of him. Bill loudly cursed the driver, but there was nothing he could do except trundle along behind the vehicle until he saw an opportunity to overtake.

He wasn't sure what he planned to do, but realised Carrie probably knew a lot from her talks with the old lady. A couple of years before, he'd made it a point to visit his mother, who told him a lot more about RT, learnt from her visits with her former daughter-in-law. Things that Carrie had said showed the old lady knew far more about a lot of influential people. People, Bill Swallow wanted to please – for the money and for his own safety. Men – and women, who were involved with money laundering, large-scale drug dealing, and many other illegal activities. Bill himself became involved with some of them during his working life in Las Vegas. Any one of them would take him out, and so he set out to please his bosses, and if it meant killing his ex-wife, he'd do it.

It was only after they passed the sign for Mammoth Lakes, Carrie became aware of a car following them. She couldn't work out whether it was really following them or just heading down the same route. If it was someone tailing them, how on earth did anyone know she was back in California? However, the feeling of fear swept over her.

"Adam, there's a car behind us, and whoever is driving it is keeping pace with us".

Adam looked back and watched it for a few minutes, and it certainly looked as if Carrie was right.

"Do you think Bill could have gone back to that coffee shop and the owner told him about a British couple coming in, and that he'd told them about the railway station?"

"I suppose it could have happened, so just keep looking ahead. I'll watch and see if he tries to overtake us."

Carrie gripped the steering wheel, "They didn't get me before and I am damned if they will this time. Adam, I'm going to try and lose that car behind us. I know this road really well, and at this time of the year, there isn't a lot of traffic. I want to try and put some yardage between us on the other car, so hang on."

For the next 15 or 20 minutes, it was fairly hair-raising, and Adam felt that he was somehow taking part in a mountain rally. But he had to give it to her, she really could drive. Sometimes he would ask her where she learnt. Another of her father's lessons?

Suddenly Carrie said, "Hold on now, I'm going to turn off the road shortly." With that, she slammed on the brakes and skidded off to the left, hoping the dust she churned up would have subsided by the time the following car drove past the entrance. Wrenching the wheel over, they turned into what was obviously a little airport. She rapidly drove the car along the side of the runway almost to the far end and stopped beside some hangars, knowing they were completely hidden by the trees and shrubs lining the side of the airport, and even if anyone drove in, they wouldn't see the car. Then she quickly turned off the engine, and they sat there in silence. Not long after that, they heard a car heading south and driving at speed.

"So, what do we do now?" asked Adam.

"We wait for a little while to see what happens. I am certain whoever it was in the other car was too far behind us to see us leave the highway".

"Then what? We can't go back onto the highway, so I guess we are stuck here for a while".

"No. We are going to steal an airplane!"

What?!"

"No, not really, we're actually just going to borrow one. There's one here that belongs to a good friend of mine, and I've flown it many times. I know where he hides the key - here just inside the gas cap."

Adam noticed that Carrie was already reverting to the American way of saying things.

As Carrie said that she opened up the cap and pulled out the key.

"While I do the pre-flight checks, Adam, please, will you grab our bags out of the car and put them behind the seats inside the airplane. I think the best thing would be to drive the car into that empty hangar behind us. Then, please just slide the door closed. If anyone comes looking for the car or us, it won't be immediately visible."

Adam shook his head at this remarkable woman and went off to do as she had asked. Before they flew south, they both needed to make some phone calls. Carrie wanted to speak to her solicitor, Gary Newsome, to tell him about what was happening and to ask him to contact Olivia and bring her to the bank at around 3.30 pm when she hoped she and Adam be there. She didn't dare call Olivia directly, because, as Adam said, it might not be safe.

"Hi Gary, I'm back in California and heading for the bank. Please can you quietly arrange for the police to be in attendance. I'm with my husband, Adam, and we will be opening up my safe deposit boxes where I've stored the old lady's things, the one who left me everything she owned. I believe, before her father had landed on a private airstrip on a ranch about 30 miles north of the Mexican border. The rancher wasn't happy, and as he had the Californian sheriff visiting him, he decided to bring the sheriff out to find out who had landed on his private strip. He and the sheriff had been discussing the problems of small planes coming over from Mexico loaded with guns, drugs, and people, and surprisingly, parakeets hidden in the wings of the aircraft, and then landing on this private dirt strip. The sheriff parked the car right in front of the aeroplane and made it impossible for Carrie's father to fly back to where the little San Juan Capistrano airstrip was.

Later, they laughed about the illegal landing, because when the sheriff had inquired as to where Carrie's father had come from, he'd replied from Southampton, England, where am I? Needless to say, the sheriff didn't find that particularly funny. After that, Buddy and Carrie's dad became firm friends. Carrie didn't actually know whether Buddy was his real name, but her dad always referred to him like that when he said they were going off to have a beer or two.

Adam called his boss, Steven, back in England to update him. He understood that someone from the British Consulate would also be joining him at the bank when they opened the boxes.

"By the way, Adam, I have put you down as officially representing the British government. This is until we can get people out there to help you."

It was obvious the British police were taking this very seriously. What Adam had said had convinced Steven that this was something that could bring governments down.

When Adam had finished hiding the car, he climbed into the seat alongside Carrie, who had completed her preflight checks. She turned the airplane round to taxi to the far end of the runway, mentally saying a big thank you to the owner of this little plane for having the tank fully filled with fuel. And it was before they took off that they both made the phone calls they needed to. Once in the air, it would have been impossible.

Back at the end of the runway, Carrie held it there while she revved up the engine before allowing the little plane to ease off the ground. Pulling back the controls, she rapidly climbed to 1500 feet and turned the nose and pointed it to the south. As they flew over the little town of Lone Pine, they saw a car making a U-turn. They had no idea if this was the car that had been following them, but were very happy to be where they were, high above the ground.

It was Bill Swallow, and he had been following them. He shook his head, surely, he would have caught up with them by now, although he had been careful not to exceed the speed limit too much. Getting pulled over by the Highway Patrol wouldn't suit him at all. He had too many questions against his name.

Bill decided they must have turned off on a track leading towards the mountains, and so he chose a bar alongside the road and sat and waited. If they had turned off, then they would at some points have come past heading south. In the meantime, he called Joel.

"Hi, Joel. She is back in the States. I've just seen her and some guy in a silver Honda Accord, with Canadian plates, and think they are heading south along Route 395. I'm guessing Carrie maybe going back to her house in South Laguna. I want you to get over there to check it out. It'll be a few hours before she arrives, go and hang out there".

"Yes, boss. What do you want me to do if they turn up?"

"Call me. Oh, I think Mungo knows where Carrie's friend lives, send him over there".

"What are you going to do?"

"The only other place she might go is the bank where she worked. Think you said that was where she twigged you had something to do with the killing of the old lady. You said she recognised a piece of jewellery – that right?"

"Yes, she did".

"What did you do with it?"

"I've got it at my apartment, hidden away".

"You stupid bastard! If the cops latch on to you and do a search, that'll be you in for life".

"I've hidden it well. I don't think they'll find it".

Bill hit back, "They will, believe me, they will".

"What are you going to do if you find her?"

"I'm leaving now to get ahead of her, leave me to figure what I'm going to do", and he hung up.

Joel did as he was told. No good upsetting the boss, he had too many friends who would think nothing of taking Joel out. Before leaving his apartment, guessing he had plenty of time to get there if she was still somewhere en route through the Sierra Nevada mountains, he called Mungo.

"Remember I told you about seeing that broad in London, the one we were supposed to take out? Somehow, she gave Bill and me the slip. She is now back in California. The boss saw her in a car driving south. He thinks she will be heading for her house in South Laguna but may try to get to her friend's." He said, "For you to go over there and wait to see if she shows up".

"What do I do if she does?"

"Call me and I will let him know".

"What if the other broad leaves her house?"

"Follow her, I guess. The boss said she was driving a silver Honda Accord with Canadian numbers. So, watch out for that as well".

Joel then headed off for Carrie's house. He remembered it well as he and Mungo had visited it several times around the time the woman had vanished.

At her house, he drove past very slowly, looking to see who might be around. A woman inside the house, Carrie's tenant, was looking out of the front window, watching for a delivery, when she saw him.

He parked a little way down the road and appeared to be settling in as if waiting for something. So, she called the police.

Joel was almost dozing off in the warm Californian sunshine when he was startled by two police cars, which parked one in front of him and the other right behind him.

"Get out!"

"What have I done?"

"Nothing yet as we know of. Get out!" said one of the cops and pulled out his gun.

Joel quickly did as he was told. where he was very roughly frisked by another of the policemen.

"Hands up on the side of your car – higher! Feet spread apart".

Of course, they found he was carrying a gun himself and removed it from his jacket. Without hesitating, he was quickly handcuffed and pushed into the back of one of the Sheriff's cars.

"Identification, License, and car docs".

"Hey, what are you doing. I ain't done nothing wrong!"

"Shut up.. You're coming with us to the station".

"But I was only sitting there enjoying the sun!"

"Not in a residential area you don't – and not carrying a weapon".

Joel almost wailed, "But nowadays everyone is loaded".

"Shut up, mister, if you don't want to get charged with something worse".

At the police station, they checked Joel out and found connections with various gangs and decided to have a look into his apartment to see what else he'd hidden; they were looking especially for more weaponry and drugs, and anything else to incriminate him. Cops don't like men like Joel hanging around residential streets in the quiet area where he was found. Burglary and paedophilia, and probably drug dealing were among other crimes he could have been involved in.

Having fingerprinted him at the police station, they ran them through their files and discovered they matched those found in the apartment of the old lady known as RT, who was brutally murdered over a year before. The names weren't the same. The man whose fingerprints had turned up at the murder scene was on file as Jose Lopez. This man was calling himself Joel Hernandez. Different names, same prints. That was going to nail him.

Joel was thoroughly searched and had everything confiscated, including his belt, before being locked into a cell. All he could think of was 'God damned Bill Swallow', he knew the broad was an ex-wife of his. He'd gotten him into this situation. Joel continued mentally to rail against his 'boss', but knew he had no option but to obey this 'son of a bitch' who could have him taken out at any moment.

Orders went out to an appropriate squad to go and search his apartment.

"Take it apart and bring in everything you find".

This was how the bracelet known as the 'Dragon's Breath' was found, and it was the final crime to send Joel to jail for life.

He squealed, of course. He tried to blame his cohorts, Mungo and Bill Swallow, and passed on their names and contact numbers in the hope it would help him. The police remained silent as they took down all the information. At that time, the police didn't know they were within touching distance of picking up all three, and a silent thank you went to the observant woman in Carrie's house.

In the meantime, Mungo was heading for Olivia's apartment. He'd been there a number of times in the past when they were trying to track down Carrie. Most of the time Olivia's car was parked out front, but today it was absent. Having hung around for an hour or so, after asking her neighbour if she had been seen that morning and got a negative, he even tried her doorbell but got no answer.

What bothered him was that he'd tried Joel's cell phone several times and didn't get any answer.

"Where the hell was he? What was he, Mungo supposed to do? He didn't know Bill Swallow's phone number; in fact, he only knew him as Bill. He thought he'd better hang on for a bit longer and try Joel again.

Olivia's phone signalled an intruder alarm. She checked her phone camera and saw a strange man just walking away from the front door. Winding the tape back, she discovered he'd been parked up for an hour or so.

So, she called the police.

Mungo was about to give up and drive away when he found himself blocked, like Joel before him, by a Sheriff's vehicle and was persuaded, much against his will, to accompany him to the nearest police station.

Meanwhile, unaware of the problem Joel and Mungo had gotten into, Bill made his way towards Laguna Hills, where he hoped to meet up with Carrie.

# Chapter 23

Carrie decided to follow route 395 as it would take them east of the massive Sierra Nevada mountains. Suddenly, to Adam's surprise, the massive mountain range ended, and they found themselves flying over the Mojave Desert. Carrie pointed out in the far distance, Edwards Air Force Base. She told Adam her father had been very friendly with one of the secret test pilots there. That was a long time ago, after her father had moved from England, and while the test pilot friend was working in the American Embassy and linked to the US Air Force.

"Whenever dad's friend, Jon, gave a cocktail party to which Russian guests were invited, the whole family had to be very careful about what they said until the house had been 'swept' for listening devices placed around by these guests. On one occasion, Jon said he knew a Russian guest was trying to get information to pass back, so Jon, just to wind him up, asked him if he remembered during WWII, when the German army tried to make it to Moscow? The Russian replied yes, so Jon quietly whispered, "We've got 50,000 Hovercraft waiting to come at you, and you are not going to stop the US!" We all laughed about the story and wondered about what had been reported back to their authorities.

Adam laughed as well.

En route, Carrie pointed out the little towns of Johannesburg and Red Mountain. These, she said, had originally been gold mining towns. She allowed the plane to drop down quite a way so that she could point out the old wooden square-faced buildings, usually only seen in the movies.

Once they reached the southern end of the Mojave Desert, she turned the little plane towards the east in order to avoid getting anywhere near the air control space around the big Los Angeles airport.

Adam could tell she was getting more tense as her hands gripped the control column tightly.

"Are you OK, Carrie?"

"Yes, I'm trying to concentrate on finding the runway. I know it can't be far now".

Suddenly, when it looked as though they were in the middle of nowhere, Carrie began the descent towards what appeared to be just scrubland and crevices criss-crossing a wild area. Adam was concerned and afraid that she must have lost her way as the ground looked treacherous. And then he noticed a strip of open ground which was obviously a landing strip.

She went through the routine, and somehow out she lined up with the open stretch of ground, and as it was a fixed-wheel plane, she had no need to worry about landing gear. She cut back on the engine speed, although for Adam it still seemed very fast, touched down, and allowed the little plane to run out towards the end of the dirt strip. Putting her feet on the brakes, she came to a halt and switched the engine off. Adam let out a sigh of relief. He'd never been in an airplane so small before, and had been very nervous, although he wouldn't dare to show it. He now realised he shouldn't have been. This wife of his was extraordinary!

As soon as she landed, a four-wheeled drive vehicle came up alongside them.

"Hi Carrie, it's good to see you, but where the hell have you been? I've asked around for you, but nobody seemed to know. You just vanished."

"I know, Buddy, it's a long story, and I'll be happy to tell you all about it when the next few hours are over. By the way, this is my husband, Adam Scott."

"Good to meet you, Adam. Now Carrie, what do you want me to do?"

"Well, first of all, I need to get this plane off the strip. Can I put it in your big barn?"

"Sure thing. Look, I brought you out a couple of mugs of coffee because I thought you'd be ready for it. And I got a bag of doughnuts for you, too."

Adam replied, "We certainly are - thank you."

After finishing their coffee, Buddy walked over to the big barn to open the large doors, followed by Adam, while Carrie manoeuvred the plane to line up with the opening. She then eased the aircraft towards the entrance to the barn before shutting down the engine and allowing the two men to guide it into place in the darkness of the building, before climbing out.

Adam collected their luggage, ready to load it into the truck, while Buddy closed the large doors of the barn to hide the airplane. He said he would contact Bruce, the owner, and let him know his plane was safely stowed at the ranch.

"I'll help him get it back north, if he needs me to".

"Thanks, Buddy, you always were a great friend to Dad".

Piling their belongings into his truck, they set off across country towards Laguna Hills and the bank. It took them a while to drive along the dirt roads to reach the highway, and during that time Carrie, sitting beside Buddy, filled him in with some of their recent history.

"Carrie, you never said anything about getting married, and how come he's a Brit?"

"It's a long and complicated story. Do you remember hearing about the murder of the old lady in Laguna Beach – getting on for two years ago?"

Buddy nodded, "I read somewhere you were involved, and at the time I was curious. After a while, I tried to call you. Was planning to ask you if you wanted to fly out to Mojave with a bunch of us over the Labor Day weekend".

"I would have loved to have come with you. Do you remember the fun times we had when Dad was alive? I always think back to the great steaks you cooked. Do you also remember the car explosion in the parking lot in Laguna Hills? That was my car".

"Gosh, Carrie! I had no idea. What happened?"

"It had to do with the murder of RT, the old lady. I accidentally found out who did it. It wasn't just a small burglary; it was connected to some pretty high-up people – going all the way to the top. I'm not saying the President was involved, but I'm guessing, from things RT told me, there were people doing things they shouldn't have been and probably guys connected with organised crime were part of it".

They chatted on for a while before Carrie became very quiet, and Adam knew she was scared or worried.

Upon arrival, it was obvious a lot was going on. Carrie suddenly felt very frightened again. There were police cars parked all around the area in front of the bank. Once they had identified themselves, they were allowed through the police cordon. Adam told her to stay in the car until he'd been over to talk to the officials. Carrie slid herself onto the floor to wait for him to come back. He told her she was safe.

What they didn't see was that another car had arrived carrying Nevada number plates. The car belonged to Bill Swallow. He tried to bluff his way in.

"What do you want?" asked the cop who was on duty near the entrance.

"My wife works here, in the bank, and she asked me to meet her. She needs a lift home", said Bill, making it up as he went along.

"Wait here a minute, Sir, I'll just check. What's her name?".

"Carrie Swallow".

It was too late for Bill Swallow to turn around and drive away. Another cop was keeping his eye on him.

The second policeman, having heard the exchange, wandered over to talk to Bill, "You from around here, sir?"

"Yes, we live in South Laguna", replied Bill, forgetting the Nevada plates.

"South Laguna? How come the number plates?"

Bill could have kicked himself, and the cop noticed the angry frown appear. Bill lied again.

"It belongs to a friend of mine. He lives in Vegas".

"Can I see your driving licence and the car documents?"

That's done it, thought Bill.

At that moment, the first cop returned. "It seems that nobody knows a Carrie Swallow round here. There used to be a woman called that, but she just disappeared one day. Also, the person I spoke to said Carrie had divorced some years back, and that she wasn't married. So, let's have the real story, shall we?".

At that moment, a more senior officer drove over. He'd had a report about someone called Joel, who was locked up, having had something to do with a murder some time back. Anyway, he was telling his story to anyone who would listen and mentioned two friends of his who were implicated – named someone called Mungo, and his boss, he said, whose name of Bill Swallow.

"You're a liar, Mr. Swallow, and not a very good one at that. Get the cuffs on him. He's coming in for more questioning".

Bill tried to talk his way out, but the police appeared not to hear him.

"Get him in the car".

A few minutes after this incident, Adam arrived back at the car, with a couple of the Californian sheriffs.

"It's alright Carrie, as you can see the police are here in their dozens and also someone from the British Consulate, and I believe the FBI and CIA have several representatives as well," Adam told her.

"At the moment, the police are evacuating the building, and once everyone is out, they will close the front door, leaving the bank's security man outside to tell people that the bank is temporarily closed due to an incident."

Word got out that something unusual was happening, and one or two press people turned up but were politely told they were getting nothing in the way of information and if they tried to publish anything, they themselves would be arrested.

Buddie's vehicle pulled up as close as he could get it to the front door in order to screen Carrie from anyone watching. As soon as she was inside, Buddy pulled away to head home, just shouting to them, "Talk to you later."

The only person left inside apart from Olivia, who, if Mungo had known it, was waiting in the bank for Carrie to arrive, and Gary Newsome, the attorney, and some pretty stern-faced men who obviously were wondering what the hell was going on. The one person still inside was Flo, and as soon as she handed over the bank's key, which had to be used, along with the key Carrie had in her pocket, in order to get into her safe deposit box.

Flo wasn't allowed to talk to Carrie, who looked so different with the change of hairstyle, she didn't immediately recognise her but was ushered out through the front door with a warning not to say anything to anybody especially the couple of pressmen who were waiting - although by the time she got out the police had shifted them. As she left, the security doorman closed the big main doors to the bank behind himself but remained outside in the hopes of seeing or hearing what was really going on.

# Chapter 24

The next phase had begun. Nobody there, apart from Carrie, had any idea what to expect.

She went to her own original safe deposit box first. Inside, they found her cell phone, credit cards, savings books, and other personal things she'd left behind when she fled the country. Inside was also the key to the other box, containing everything RT had given her. The officials cleared some desks, and as things were pulled out, they laid them out in order to go through them carefully. The FBI men, Carrie's attorney, and Adam, on behalf of the British government, along with the man from the British Consulate, began carefully going through them one by one.

Inside, they found journals, letters, papers, and lots of photographs linking her to the organised crime perpetrators she'd described. The men looking through these could hardly believe their eyes. Some of the crimes were linked to the people they were looking at, both men and women, with staggering. They knew this was going to be an enormous job and would probably take months, if not years, to catch up with some of these people. One or two of them had made huge sums of money and were now hiding out on their own private islands in the Caribbean. Others would be found in places like New York, Las Vegas and Chicago. Many of them, they suspected, had multiple hideouts and property not only in the United States but in parts of South America as well, South Africa, and across Europe and the Far East.

Olivia, who wasn't needed in the search but was allowed to stay to support Carrie, made herself useful in making numerous cups of coffee for the men investigating the staggering amount of incriminating information they were pulling out. As they went through it, they were not surprised to find that RT had been murdered. The information and knowledge of people in higher places who had been involved with fraud, trafficking, money laundering, corruption, and interference with other countries' Governments, and also murders, astonished them. Many of the past murders were still being investigated, but it seemed as though they might now have evidence to go after the perpetrators. They knew they had a very big job ahead of them to bring those to justice who were still alive.

Joel Hernandez who obviously was not very intelligent had stupidly for himself, had completed the form when he applied for the safe deposit box, giving his own name and his address. Carrie pulled that out quickly, and the officials confirmed he was already in custody.

Later, to Carrie's delight, she was informed they had recovered the precious Dragon's Breath bracelet from Joel's apartment.

When he'd been arrested, he was very quick to implicate the Irishman Mungo Fisher. He told them that it was actually Mungo who had done the murder, but admitted that he had been involved in the ransacking of the old lady's apartment. He also mentioned Bill Swallow, who was their boss, and like Mungo, was living in Las Vegas.

The police had already picked up Mungo and arrested him. He was also definitely going away for the rest of his life, if the death penalty wasn't imposed upon him.

They found links between Joel's phone and Bill Swallow's, which incriminated the three of them as being associates.

Eventually, hours later, the officials gathered all the papers they'd pulled out of RT's box. Gary Newsome, Carrie's attorney, had been allowed to take notes of what had been found, but not photographs.

Olivia offered to take Carrie and Adam back to her house for the night. The police arranged for armed patrols to guard the house, 24 hours a day.

Exhausted, at almost midnight, everyone left the building. Every piece of paper and document had been carefully photographed and numbered before being countersigned by the officials and Carrie's attorney, Gary.

Before the morning, many criminals had been rudely awakened and arrested, not only in the United States, but everywhere, in Europe, the Far East, and places like Hawaii. The police had to go in swiftly and without it being obvious in order to stop information from being circulated to other criminals around the world. Some of these people were very highly ranked in police forces, politicians, and even royal families were not exempt.

Armed with the key and the code belonging to the other boxes left in RT's possession and lodged in the vault in Philadelphia, a few days after the raid on the safe deposit box in Laguna Hills, containing the documents Carrie had locked in her possession, Adam and Carrie were flown to Philadelphia to search the files and boxes which had been hidden for many years and which RT had been told were her passport to use as blackmail should she ever need money.

There were only American enforcement agents with them this time.

RT was correct, the boxes contained documents and details that would take weeks to sift through. They were dynamite, RT had confided to Carrie, and had she done as suggested and threatened to expose some of the secrets hidden away for many years, she could have netted many millions of dollars. She had never done so. Carrie thought back to things RT had told her and believed she'd known how and why her senator had died. Later, after the papers and stuffed envelopes had been perused, it was confirmed that someone with a grudge against him had indeed been involved with his murder.

Most of the information was long out of date, and although the information answered many questions, there were few of the original people left to cause much harm to.

It appeared that the whole organisation was controlled by one family, originally from Ireland. They were known as the Irish American Mafia, brutal, ruthless, and happy to take out anyone who interfered, especially other gangs who tried to muscle in on their perceived territory. Few people knowing them would have ever guessed they had so much power. Many of them ran small family businesses to conceal the true extent of the web of deceit, which crossed many countries, especially the United States. They virtually controlled Las Vegas, which is where Bill Swallow became involved, and this is why he was caught up and was now serving a life sentence. This gang had enforcers in the jails, and he lasted less than a year inside.

Carrie and Adam questioned why RT hadn't been killed many years before and the only conclusion they came to was that she had been the mistress of the big boss of the cartel and even after they were no longer together he still seemed to have a fondness for her – hence his gift of all the documents with the instructions to use any of it if she needed money. Then he died and she became vulnerable.

# Chapter 25

After several weeks of going to meetings and attending official formalities, Adam and Carrie knew that they had to return to England at least for a while. Adam had already told his boss, Steven French, of his plans to retire from the force in the next few months.

This time, they flew back in a private jet. The Chief Inspector had arranged for them to be collected at the airport and taken home. After the driver of the car unloaded their bags and said goodbye. With happy tears in her eyes, Carrie smiled at Adam as they entered their home.

Two days later, Adam met up with his boss, Steven French, to discuss everything that had gone on. He knew he was going to have to attend many meetings with people like MI5 and had already been asked to go to 10 Downing Street to meet up with the Prime Minister and other top civil servants. Carrie's old lady, RT, had so much information about people in high places that it was going to be quite a long time to catch up with those involved. Many of these people denied all knowledge, and quite a number of barristers and legal advisors began raking in huge sums of money for themselves. Some of these people had died – many in suspicious circumstances.

Adam's mother, Anne, came to visit them very soon after they arrived back from the States and gave them both big hugs. She was in tears with relief that they had returned safely, and a few weeks later, when she discovered she was going to be a grandmother, she was almost off her head with excitement.

Carrie also came in for her fair share of questioning and discussions during transatlantic communications, after all she was the one RT had confided in. While Adam got on with winding things up at work, Carrie quietly went about sorting things out at home.

Carrie took Adam to meet her godmother, who lived just outside Salcombe, and that was when they learned about the godmother's nonreaction to the plea for information about Carrie. She said that as she was in the middle of the Mediterranean on her way to Australia and New Zealand, she had no idea anyone was searching for her.

It was about six months later that they felt they could return to California. In the meantime, Adam's boss had told him he had decided to retire as well. The Chief Inspector, Steven, quietly said that he had heard on the Grapevine that he himself was to get an honour in the New Year's honours list and that Adam was going to get an MBE. Adam disputed this and said that it was Carrie who deserved the recognition, not himself.

So, some seven months after James and Carrie returned to England, they flew out again, along with his mother, Anne, who was planning to stay with them until after her first grandchild was born. This time they went as Mr and Mrs Scott, albeit Adam was MBE.

Carrie had talked regularly to Olivia, and it was she who came to collect them from the airport and drive them home. Olivia and Anne happily discussed the upcoming inevitable baby shower, with Anne enthusiastically throwing herself into all the arrangements.

Olivia and Carrie chatted about the wedding of Olivia and Carrie's attorney, Gary Newsome. This was due to take place about five months after the birth of Carrie's baby. The four younger people became even closer as friends.

Carrie and James, and his mother took a trip to June Lake to look for a cabin they could buy. As they passed the entrance to Bishop Airport, they both looked at each other and thought back to the day when Carrie had 'borrowed' a plane.

They found a cabin they all loved. It was a little way beyond June Lake itself, but close to the ski slopes for the winter.

Back in South Laguna, three or four months after the baby had been born, Gary sat down with Carrie and James and went through all the paperwork and finances that he'd handled on her behalf while she'd been missing for nearly a year. Carrie was astonished by the amount of money RT had left her, and it made her a very wealthy woman. The sale of RT's house had been considerable because of its location in the older part of Laguna Beach. RT's attorney had worked closely with Gary and had turned up a number of other bank accounts that she hadn't disclosed to Carrie.

They were able to buy, as well as the very nice cabin in June Lake, a larger property in South Laguna, more suitable for bringing up a family. This had to have views across the Pacific Ocean and out towards Catalina Island. Carrie had insisted it had a deck where they could sit in the evening with a glass of wine for her and a beer for Adam. From here, they could watch the sun sink until it looked as though it was disappearing into the water.

They decided to keep Carrie's smaller cottage for Anne to move into. She was, by this time, becoming more Californian by the day. She looked back and realised that her life in southern Devon had been rather dull, whereas there were so many fun things to do, and also, to be near her family was an easy choice to make.

Although they were feted by many people, they preferred to socialise with their family and close friends.

The former Chief Inspector, Steven French, who kept in touch regularly with James, had told them to prepare themselves for an invasion of his family when they came to visit the Scott's the following year.

Adam, although officially retired, was regularly called upon by the British police if they needed to make enquiries about British citizens living in the US.

Among the many things they had retrieved from RT's home were many bound books, which had filled up quite a lot of one of her bookshelves. These contained handwritten journals and photograph albums dating back to the early years of her life and those of her family. Photographs of the family home in Rhode Island fascinated them both. Pictures of ladies dressed in what Anne described as Edwardian dresses, horse-drawn carriages, balls, and family picnics were all totally enthralling. But by far the best, as far as Carrie was concerned, were those of RT herself. To say she was striking as a young woman was evident, and Carrie could quite understand why the young men flocked around her. In some ways, Carrie felt a little sad she hadn't married and had her own family, but then again, what would the world have missed without such a colourful character!

Fortunately, Joel and Mungo hadn't noticed these when they ransacked her house, but then they weren't looking for them and wouldn't have been interested. Adam and Carrie found the albums full of former social history, and among them, newspaper cuttings and photographs from social glossy magazines were all there to catalogue her life. They told so many stories about this enterprising and extraordinary woman. Later photographs contained pictures of RT, her senator lover, and many of the most notorious people, not only from the United States but other countries as well.

They didn't know it, but RT had planned to tell Carrie all about these books and albums, but her untimely death stopped this from happening.

Carrie had her Dragon's breath bracelet back. It had been found in Joel's apartment when the police ransacked it soon before the opening of the safe deposit boxes.

While she and Adam were enjoying a quieter life with their new son, whom they had named after Carrie's father, they were in unison about turning RT's journals and life story into a book which they planned to call 'The Senator's Mistress: The woman who knew too much'

The end.

www.ingramcontent.com/pod-product-compliance
Lightning Source LLC
Chambersburg PA
CBHW020804310726
48969CB00002B/691